Evangeline Mudd

and the
Golden-Haired
Apes of the
Ikkinasti Jungle

DAVID ELLIOTT

ILLUSTRATED BY
ANDRÉA WESSON

CANDLEWICK PRESS
CAMBRIDGE, MASSACHUSETTS

*Behind every book there is an author, but behind
every author there is an editor. A good editor can look into a
wilderness and see a garden. Liz Bicknell is just such an editor.
Thank you, Liz. As Dadoo might say, you really are
most extremely greats and wonderfuls.*
D. E.

Text copyright © 2004 by David Elliott
Illustrations copyright © 2004 by Andréa Wesson

First paperback edition 2007

The Library of Congress has cataloged the hardcover edition
as follows:
Elliott, David, date.
Evangeline Mudd and the golden-haired apes of the Ikkinasti Jungle / by David Elliott ;
illustrated by Andréa Wesson. — 1st ed.
p. cm.
Summary: When Evangeline Mudd's primatologist parents travel without her to the
Ikkinasti Jungle to study the golden-haired apes, Evangeline and the world-famous Dr.
Aphrodite Pikkaflee are eventually called upon to rescue the Mudds and save the jungle
from the evil schemes of Aphrodite's money-mad brother.
ISBN 978-0-7636-1876-6 (hardcover)
[1. Jungles—Fiction. 2. Primates—Fiction. 3. Humorous stories.]
I. Wesson, Andréa, ill. II. Title.
PZ7.E447Ev 2004
[Fic]—dc21 2003043775

ISBN 978-0-7636-2614-3 (paperback)

2 4 6 8 10 9 7 5 3 1

Printed in the United States of America

This book was typeset in Plantin.

Candlewick Press
2067 Massachusetts Avenue
Cambridge, Massachusetts 02140

visit us at www.candlewick.com

To Emma and Lily Panish

Chapter 1

The Luckiest Girl in the World

Evangeline Mudd thought she was the luckiest girl in the world, and who knows? Perhaps she was. After all, how many of you have parents who not only *let* you swing from the chandeliers but *teach* you to do it? How many of you have parents who play for hours and hours on end, chasing and somersaulting and rolling around on the soft earth like chimpanzees? And how many of you have parents who say things like, "Oh, don't bother taking a bath tonight, dear. You just had one last week." Probably none of you, I'm sorry to say. Unless of course, your parents are *primatologists,* which is exactly what Evangeline Mudd's parents were.

Now, in case you don't know it, primatologists are people who study monkeys and apes and, yes, even human beings. You've probably seen them on television. They're usually mucking around a jungle somewhere, whispering into microphones so as not to irritate the five-hundred-pound gorilla sitting next to them. They also use fancy words like *brachiate*. (If you don't know the meaning of that word, don't worry. You'll learn all about it in the next chapter.)

Evangeline's parents, Dr. Merriweather and Dr. Magdalena Mudd, didn't know much about gorillas, but they did know almost everything there was to know about the golden-haired apes of the Ikkinasti Jungle. Merriweather and Magdalena had spent their entire lives studying the golden-hairs. They knew what the golden-hairs ate. They knew where the golden-hairs slept. They even knew what the golden-hairs thought was funny and what the golden-hairs considered to be in poor taste. Yes, the golden-haired apes of the Ikkinasti Jungle, known throughout the world of primatology for their harmonious way of life and their fun-loving temperaments, were the Mudds' specialty.

(By the way, all primatologists have specialties. That is, some primatologists know everything there is to know about the Madagascar aye-aye and not a thing about the blue-eyed lemur. Others can tell you what the red-bottomed baboon eats for breakfast, but wouldn't know a golden potto if one knocked on their door and tried to sell them the Hoopty-Doopty Deluxe Vacuum complete with all attachments.)

But what does all this have to do with Evangeline, you might be asking yourself. What does all this have to do with Evangeline Mudd, the luckiest girl in the world? The answer to that question is quite simply *everything*.

You see, not long before Evangeline was born, Merriweather and Magdalena came to an important decision, a decision that only primatologists could have made.

They were sitting in the garden of their little bungalow in the woods of New England. When they weren't tramping around the jungles of Ikkinasti, Merriweather and Magdalena lived in this bungalow, and it was here that they planned to raise their new baby.

"Magdalena, my dear?" Merriweather had said.

He was a tall man, and very thin. Lying as he was in the garden chaise, he looked all arms and legs and put one in mind of the insect commonly known as the walking stick.

"Yes, Merriweather, my darling?" Magdalena answered dreamily.

It was nearing the end of the day, and the roses and heliotropes and lilies were blooming so profusely and their scent was so heavy upon the air that Magdalena felt as if she were being hypnotized by the sheer loveliness of it all. Magdalena herself was a short woman, and quite plump, especially since the baby was due to arrive any day. With her curly red hair and her freckly round face, she might have been a ladybug plopped down lazily in the grass.

"I have been thinking," Merriweather continued. "I have been thinking that the golden-hair way of life, peaceful as it is, is far superior to the way that most of humankind spends its days."

"I agree, my darling," whispered Magdalena sleepily. "I agree completely."

As she finished the sentence, a giant swallowtail alighted upon her knee and slowly flapped its black-and-yellow wings.

"Look," Magdalena whispered. "It's *Papilio cresphontes.*"

Generally, primatologists know the Latin names of things. If you and I were to see a wiener dog, for example, we would call it that. But a primatologist is much more likely to say something like, "What a charming *Canis vulgaris hot doggum* you are walking, Madam." That's just how they are.

Careful not to disturb the butterfly, Merriweather took a long drink of lemonade and passed the glass over to his wife. He was still thinking about the golden-haired apes and the agreeable way in which they lived.

"Most people spend far too much time zigging . . . ," he continued.

"And zagging," Magdalena added, taking a sip of the lemonade.

"Coming . . ."

"And going."

"To-ing . . ."

"And fro-ing."

"Therefore," Merriweather continued, "I think we should raise *our* baby exactly the way golden-hair mothers and fathers raise *their* babies."

For a moment all was quiet. Not a sound could be heard except for the buzzing of the bees that were at work in the lavender and the hollyhocks. It was so quiet, in fact, that Merriweather wondered if his wife had dozed off.

"So what do you think, my dear?" Merriweather asked at last.

"What do I think?" answered Magdalena, who hadn't been asleep at all but instead had been watching the clouds sail by in great drifts of white and pink. "Why, I agree, of course. I agree completely. In fact, my darling, I had been thinking the same thing."

Throughout this conversation, the swallowtail had remained on Magdalena's knee. But now, with one lazy flap of its papery wings, it took to the air.

Presently Magdalena began again.

"Merriweather, my darling?" she said.

"Yes, Magdalena, my dear?" he answered.

"I was wondering. In all our hours of observing the golden-haired apes of the Ikkinasti Jungle, did you ever happen to see one playing the piano?"

Merriweather stopped to think for a moment. This was not a question he had been expecting.

"No," he finally answered. "I don't believe that I did. Why do you ask?"

Magdalena sighed. The trumpet lily near her slowly wagged its heavy, fragrant head.

"I did so want our child to learn the piano," she replied.

Merriweather stood up and stretched his arms over his head. They were such long arms that it seemed with very little effort he could have stretched out his fingers and taken great handfuls of the sky.

"Oh, we'll have to make exceptions here and there," he said. "Piano playing should be one of them."

"Merriweather," Magdalena said once more.

"What is it this time, my dear? Are you also thinking our child should play the flugelhorn? The glockenspiel? The double-barreled euphonium?"

"No," Magdalena replied calmly. "It's just that, well, perhaps you had better call the doctor."

Merriweather ran to the house. But before the doctor could arrive, the baby was born right there in the garden. After all, if you are going to be raised like a golden-haired ape, you might as well be born like one, too, out in the open air. The baby was a girl, a beautiful, healthy baby girl. Her parents named her Evangeline.

Eventually, the doctor did arrive. A stodgy, old-fashioned type, he did not generally approve of the way primatologists did things and insisted that Magdalena and the new baby move into the bedroom of the cozy bungalow. By the time the mother and baby were settled in, the sun was just beginning to go down. Its reds and oranges and purples reflected softly on the walls in the tidy room. It seemed as if the whole world were glowing with happiness.

As the baby was about to close her eyes, a *Papilio cresphontes* (remember?) flew into the room through the open window. Though Magdalena and Merriweather had no way of knowing it, the butterfly was the same one that earlier in the afternoon had settled upon Magdalena's knee. It fluttered for a few minutes over the baby's head and finally settled down on her foot.

Evangeline herself, young as she was, seemed delighted by the butterfly. She wriggled her tiny toes in a kind of greeting.

"Look," whispered Magdalena to her husband. "The butterfly is giving Evangeline a blessing."

With that, the little family fell asleep.

Now, in order to have a big adventure, you don't have to be born in a garden or blessed by a butterfly. Good heavens, no! In fact, I know of many adventurers who were born in great, gloomy hospitals where the nearest garden is miles away. And I know of other adventurers who are absolutely allergic to insects of all kinds, butterflies included. But when you *do* begin your life in such an extraordinary way, when you *are* born in a garden and blessed by a butterfly, extraordinary things are bound to happen to you—especially when your parents are primatologists.

Chapter 2

Life Is Perfect

As Evangeline grew, Merriweather and Magdalena realized that it would be impossible to raise her *exactly* the way golden-hair parents would. She was, after all, a human being and not an ape, and certain concessions had to be made. Diapers, for example. Naturally, golden-hair parents wouldn't dream of putting a diaper on their baby. Why would they? But Magdalena and Merriweather soon discovered that if Evangeline didn't wear diapers, well, *you* live with a big bouncing baby who doesn't wear diapers and see how *you* like it. It was just too messy.

There were other problems, too. It will not surprise you, for instance, to learn that golden-haired apes do not use knives and forks (though occasionally one might pull a grub out of a tree with a stick, which, when you think of it, isn't so very different from using a fork). In fact, I might as well tell you that the table manners of the typical golden-hair are of the kind that *some* people frown on. They eat with their feet! Not every meal, mind you, but if the occasion arises when they are swinging from tree to tree and they need their hands to hold on to the vines, their feet come in rather handy for snatching a banana and eating it on the run.

Early on, Magdalena and Merriweather agreed that this might be a very useful skill for Evangeline to acquire, and so by the time she was three years old, she could eat a peanut-butter-and-jelly sandwich with one foot and take a drink of milk with the other, all without spilling a single drop.

Later, however, this ability proved to be more trouble than it was worth, and the Mudds came to regret their decision. You see, when Evangeline was five and attending a preschool near the cozy bungalow, she ate her entire lunch with her feet so that she could have her hands free for coloring. The other children thought this such a nifty trick that they immediately ripped off their shoes and socks and tried it themselves. The result was a lot of spilled milk and sticky toes, not to mention sprained muscles of various kinds. In the end, the parents of the other children accused Evangeline of starting a foot-eating rebellion and threatened to hire lawyers if she didn't stop at once.

In spite of these difficulties, however, Merriweather and Magdalena stuck to their word and taught Evangeline the ways of the golden-hair as best they could. They knew, for example, that golden-hair youngsters learn almost everything there is to know about life by imitating their parents, and so whenever Evangeline woke up from a nap, she saw that her parents were almost always in the company of a book. The result was that by the time she was four she could read as well as any third-grader, or almost as well, at least.

Merriweather and Magdalena also knew that a big part of a golden-hair's education was learning how to solve problems. The Ikkinasti Jungle was a dangerous place, and it was absolutely necessary that a young golden-hair learn to think his way out of the hundreds of sticky situations that he could find himself in. Therefore, the Mudds devised all kinds of complicated games with their daughter involving locked boxes and keys and sweets. Within a very short time, Evangeline demonstrated just how clever she was, and before her parents knew it, she was devising games for *them*.

Of course, not everything was about learning (not that anything is wrong with learning, mind you). Not at all. In fact, one of the primary reasons that Merriweather and Magdalena loved the golden-hairs was their sense of fun. It was what they were most famous for. Unlike their cousins the gorillas, who always seemed to be irritated about something, or their other cousins the orangutans, who appeared to spend a great deal of their time thinking sad, faraway thoughts, the golden-haired apes of the Ikkinasti Jungle seemed positively dedicated to the idea that life should be jolly. They demonstrated their conviction to this philosophy by spending the best part of each day swinging through the treetops.

Yes, it seemed to Merriweather and Magdalena that the golden-hairs were among the happiest creatures on Earth, and it was this sense of contentment and merriment that they most wanted to pass along to their daughter.

"We must do all we can to prevent Evangeline from growing into one of those children who spout facts and figures but who never laugh or smile," Magdalena said one day to her husband.

"I agree, my dear," Merriweather replied. "*Those* kind of children almost always grow into *that* kind of adult."

"Too dreary," continued Magdalena.

"Far too dreary," agreed Merriweather.

That is why on Evangeline's sixth birthday her parents planned a special surprise.

The three were in the garden, very near the exact spot where Evangeline had been born. They had just finished a game of knuckle-walk tag, and Evangeline was sitting in the grass between her mother and father, humming a little tune she had made up and studying an ant that was marching up and down her thumb.

She was the perfect combination of her two parents, neither very tall, like her father, nor very short, like her mother. Her hair was a mass of tiny dark curls, no bigger around than those springs that you see in watches. They bounced cheerfully around her face with even the slightest movement of her head. Her nose was perhaps just the tiniest bit too small. Still, it had grown just where a nose should grow, and her mouth, pink as a rose, was settled perfectly under it. But the most amazing feature in her young face were her eyes. They were dark, almost black, and in them the light of both the sun and the moon seemed to have found a place to rest.

"Evangeline," her father said. "Now that you are six, your mother and I have come to an important decision."

"What is it, Merry?" she asked.

Sometimes the girl addressed her father as "Father"; at other times, she simply called him by the nickname she had given him, Merry.

"We have decided," her father replied, "that the time has come for you to learn to *brachiate*."

(Remember? I told you that you would learn the meaning of that word, and now you are about to do it.)

Evangeline's heart skipped a beat in anticipation.

"Really?" she asked, jumping up. "Do you mean it?"

"Come along, Evangeline, darling," her mother said.

Magdalena led Evangeline into the cozy bungalow, which to the girl's utter amazement and joy had been rigged from room to room with trapezes. The ceiling of that bungalow looked like the canopy of a circus tent, except there were hundreds of trapezes instead of just two or three.

"Happy birthday, darling," said Magdalena, rubbing noses with her daughter, the golden-hair way of demonstrating deep affection.

"Have a ball, my dear," said Evangeline's father, and picking her up, he extended his long arms until Evangeline took hold of one of the trapezes.

Evangeline grabbed the trapeze with both hands and pumped her legs. Within seconds the trapeze was swinging back and forth like the pendulum on a grandfather clock. Without a word from her mother or father, she grabbed the trapeze hanging directly in front of her with one hand and let go of the first trapeze with the other. In the wink of an eye, she was brachiating around the room like crazy.

Have you guessed what brachiate means yet? Yes! It's how gorillas and orangutans and chimpanzees and lots of primates, including the golden-haired ape of the Ikkinasti Jungle, get around—by swinging on vines and branches from tree to tree. It's a blast! (But don't try it without a net.)

"Wheeeeeee," called Evangeline as she zipped over and around her parents. "Watch this!"

And letting go with both hands she did a somersault before she grabbed the next trapeze.

"She's a natural," her father said proudly as he watched Evangeline whiz around the room.

"It's like she's done it all her life," Magdalena added.

In truth, Evangeline *had* brachiated before. She had been secretly practicing in the tall trees that surrounded the cozy bungalow. You mustn't think that this was any kind of naughtiness on her part. It

16

was instead the natural result of her upbringing. You see, golden-haired apes teach their children to trust their own instincts. They have to. If they didn't, how would the young apes ever survive in such a perilous place as the Ikkinasti Jungle? Since Evangeline had been raised like a golden-hair, when she realized that she was strong enough to brachiate, she naturally took to the trees. Wouldn't you have if you had been raised in such a way?

"Come on up!" she called out to her parents. "It's lovely!"

The girl did not have to wait long for her parents to join her, and before you could spell *prehensile*, Evangeline and her mother and her father were flying through the upper air of the bungalow. Once Evangeline even surprised herself by flying out of the living-room window, making a one-hundred-and-eighty-degree turn, and grabbing the trapeze closest to the window in the dining room.

Magdalena, herself an expert brachiator, followed right along behind her.

"Life is perfect!" the girl shouted through her laughter. "Absolutely perfect!"

And for a moment, time seemed to stand still as the whole world sang out in answer. *Yes! Yes! It is perfect!*

But if you had been there, you might have heard a

hint of melancholy in that answer, too, for by revolving on its axis day after day, year after year, century after century, it was as if the world had learned that perfection is a fleeting thing and does not last forever.

Chapter 3

Yes!... Yes!... Yes!... Yes!

Evangeline's musical education began not long after her sixth birthday. Merriweather had not forgotten his promise to Magdalena that Evangeline would learn to play the piano, and Evangeline herself was eager for the lessons. When she wasn't brachiating or reading, she used a pair of wooden spoons to bang out intricate rhythms on the pots and pans that her mother set out for her in the kitchen of the cozy bungalow.

From the moment she saw her, Evangeline was captivated by her piano teacher. Madame Valentina Kloudishkaya was a small woman with pale blue eyes, a huge mouth, and a beaky nose, a nose highlighted by the plumed turbans she always wore. With her matching caftans rustling and shushing whenever she moved, she looked much more like a wizard than a piano teacher.

And in a way, she was.

At Evangeline's first lesson, Madame Kloudishkaya sat her down at the piano and told her to play something. This piano, whose wing-shaped lid soared to the ceiling in a kind of permanent salute, had been made especially for the teacher, a gift from a Russian prince who had fallen madly in love with her the first time he heard her play "Chopsticks." It was the most extraordinary object Evangeline had ever seen.

Its white keys were inlaid with mother-of-pearl, and its black keys were carved of the finest ebony. Its pedals, which were suspended from an elaborate scroll, were plated with gold, and its black case, which gleamed so brilliantly in Madame Kloudishkaya's living room, had been lacquered and polished by a master of that ancient art. To Evangeline, who sat on the piano's bench in her tennis shoes and shorts, her feet barely reaching the pedals, the instrument seemed the work of a magician.

But though she seemed so plain and the piano seemed so marvelous, the girl was not intimidated. After all, zipping around the treetops is not for the timid of heart, so when Madame Kloudishkaya said, "Vell, let's see vhat you can do, tchild," Evangeline raised her hands over the keys without the slightest hesitation and let fly.

She played high. She played low. She tinkled and trilled and twittered the keys. She pounded and pummeled and thumped and thwacked. An observer might have supposed that Evangeline was engaged in some kind of battle in which it was necessary to get every possible sound out of that piano before either she or the instrument exploded. The result wasn't exactly music, but it wasn't just noise either. It was instead something totally original, rather like Evangeline herself.

The girl continued in this manner for an

exhausting three minutes, after which time, lifting her hands high over her head, she ended her performance with one tremendous and unnameable chord whose vibrations actually set the plume on Madame Kloudishkaya's turban aflutter. As the chord died away, Evangeline sat perspiring and panting as if she had just run the race of her life. She had never experienced anything like that before. She hadn't even known she was going to do it.

Throughout Evangeline's piano playing, if that's what it could be called, Madame Kloudishkaya had stood at the window, arms folded into the sleeves of her caftan, watching the girl. Her face showed not the slightest emotion, but under that caftan, her heart was beating wildly.

Once the final note of that last chord died away, she spoke.

"Zat vas ze vurst racket I haf herdt in my life!" she said. "Ze neighbors haf propaply called ze police!"

What she didn't say was that Evangeline's tone was nothing short of miraculous and that she knew pianists who had studied years to get the difficult, nearly impossible rhythms that Evangeline had played instinctively.

Of course she didn't tell Evangeline this. Madame

Kloudishkaya was a wise woman. She knew the dangers of too much praise too early. But she was eager to get started with the girl.

"Zeeze handts!" she exclaimed in spite of herself. "How didt you get zeeze shtrong handts?" she asked.

"By brachiating, probably," the girl answered.

"Ya, vell, vutefer zat is, keep doingk it," the teacher replied.

With each lesson the girl showed more discipline and more control. In no time at all, Evangeline was playing Bach fugues and Mozart sonatas. She was playing boogie-woogie and jazz and hip-hop and hop-hip and, well, there was just no kind of music the girl didn't love or couldn't play. She was even beginning to make small compositions of her own.

Sometimes, Evangeline would try to explain to her parents how she felt when she was playing the piano.

"It's like brachiating," she would say, "only with my *heart*."

By now, Evangeline was nine years old. Merriweather and Magdalena had had to make more and more concessions regarding their plan to raise their daughter. School, of course, was one of them. Still, the Mudds had done a pretty good job of it, and the little threesome was as happy as could be.

Evenings in the cozy bungalow were delightful, with Evangeline at the piano, and her mother, who was an excellent artist, sketching golden-hairs, and her father reading and studying. Occasionally, one of the three would sneak up on the others, and before you knew it, they were tickling and chasing and flying around the room like three, well, like three golden-haired apes of the Ikkinasti Jungle.

They were engaged in just exactly this kind of monkey-play when the phone call came. Now, I don't know about you, but I don't care much for phone calls. They usually come at the worst possible times, like when you are about to take your first bite of the butterscotch sundae that you had been dreaming of all day, or when you are about to beat your cousin at Go Fish and you know the minute you get up to answer the phone, he'll cheat and rig the deck. Be that as it may, when the phone rings, someone usually feels obliged to answer it. In this case, it was Evangeline's father.

"Yes?" her father said, holding the phone with one hand and grooming himself with the other. "Yes! . . . Yes! . . . Yes! . . . Yes!"

Evangeline couldn't imagine what was causing her father to yes so. Whatever it was seemed to be good news. She knew this because he was beginning to shift his weight from one foot to the other and wag his head just the way a golden-hair might do if he were being told that a shipment of gourmet bananas was on the way.

But this phone call had nothing to do with bananas. It probably would have been better if it had. For though Evangeline didn't know it, the minute that telephone rang, it set into motion a series of events that would change her life completely.

Chapter 4

You Tell Her

B y the time Merriweather hung up the phone, he was practically exploding with excitement.

"My dears!" he shouted to Magdalena and Evangeline. "You will never, never in a million years guess who that was."

"Well, my darling," Magdalena replied calmly, "if we'll never guess, then it's probably best if you tell us."

Evangeline and her mother were sitting on the floor. When the phone rang, they had been having a contest to see who could get tickled the longest without laughing. So far, Evangeline was winning.

"Dr. Aphrodite Pikkaflee!" Merriweather declared.

Magdalena jumped up from the floor like a jack-in-the-box does when you get to the *pop!* Evangeline jumped up right along with her.

"*The* Dr. Aphrodite Pikkaflee?" Evangeline asked her father.

"The very same," Merriweather replied.

Dr. Aphrodite Pikkaflee was as well known in the Mudd household as Santa Claus or George Washington is in yours. Why? She was simply the most famous primatologist in the world, that's all. If it were possible for anyone to know more about the golden-haired ape than Magdalena and Merriweather Mudd, it would be Dr. Aphrodite Pikkaflee. Some people said she was practically a golden-hair herself!

Merriweather and Magdalena had read every word of Dr. Pikkaflee's famous book, *Going Bananas: At Home with the Golden-Haired Apes of the Ikkinasti Jungle*. In fact, many of the principles upon which Evangeline herself had been raised were taken from this mighty tome. And now the great primatologist had called them. But why?

"A new group of golden-hairs has been sighted in the Ikkinasti Jungle!" Merriweather explained breathlessly. "And Dr. Aphrodite Pikkaflee, *the* Dr. Aphrodite Pikkaflee, wants *us* to go there and study them."

"Us?" Magdalena exclaimed. "But isn't she going herself?"

"Broke her leg," Merriweather said matter-of-factly. "Fell out of her nest."

He went on to explain that until her accident Dr. Pikkaflee had been living and sleeping in the treetops themselves as part of her research.

"It's for two weeks," Merriweather said. "Just think! Two weeks living with a new family of golden-hairs in the Ikkinasti Jungle."

"It's a dream come true," Magdalena replied.

Evangeline was just as excited as her parents. Having been raised so much like a golden-hair, going to the Ikkinasti Jungle would practically be like going home.

"When do we leave?" she asked. "Hadn't we better start packing?"

But something was wrong, terribly wrong. She knew it instantly from the way that her father was looking at her mother and the way that her mother was looking back at her father. It was as if each were silently saying to the other, "You tell her," and the other was responding just as silently with, "I can't! You tell her!"

Magdalena knelt down beside her daughter.

"The Ikkinasti Jungle is a dangerous place, darling," she said. "A very dangerous place. There are little wormy things that crawl between your toes. They enter your bloodstream and turn you the color of a ripe plum."

"I'll wear boots!" Evangeline replied. "Thick boots that the little wormy things can't get through."

"There are mosquitoes the size of hummingbirds," said Merriweather, kneeling down so that he could be closer to Evangeline. "Remember Professor Horvitzstein-Klein?" he said to his wife, who sighed and nodded.

"Who was that?" Evangeline asked. "That Professor Horsewich . . ."

"Horvitzstein-Klein," Magdalena corrected.

"Yes," continued Evangeline. "Who was that? That Professor Horvitzstein-Klein? What happened to him?"

"*Her,*" said Merriweather. "Professor Swoozie Horvitzstein-Klein was a primatologist, just like we are. She went into the Ikkinasti Jungle, and a swarm of those mosquitoes attacked her until she scratched herself into one big oozing blob."

"Even her own mother didn't recognize her," Magdalena said sadly.

"Finally, she just oozed away," Merriweather said. "She just oozed away until there was nothing left of her."

"I'll bring bug spray," Evangeline declared. "Professor Horvitzstein-Klein should have, too."

"But, darling," Magdalena said, gently parting Evangeline's curls and inspecting her scalp in a way that always soothed the girl when she was excited or upset. "What about the spiders? Have you forgotten about the spitting spiders?"

Evangeline had *not* forgotten about the spiders. In fact, the minute she thought she would be going to the Ikkinasti Jungle, ninety-nine percent of her was ready to leave that instant, but one percent of her was already thinking about those spiders. Her parents had often told her about them, and she herself had read more than once the passage in Dr. Pikkaflee's book:

The spitting spiders of the Ikkinasti Jungle are as big as dinner plates. Their webs are the size of doors. A fiery red, you feel you absolutely must get a look at them, but if you do, look out! They are as ferocious as they are beautiful. They let loose with a big glob of spidery spit that lands right in your eyes. That spit has special blinding powers. You can't see a thing! You wander around in circles hoping to escape, but it's too late! One by one, they move in on you, and before you can say Little Miss Muffet, they've got you wound up in a web so tight you can't even move your pinkie. After that, you're the spiders' idea of Thanksgiving—turkey, stuffing, and pumpkin pie!

"I don't care," she said. "I'm not scared of any old spiders."

Now, there are times in life when you have to say what you think *might be* true in the future rather than what actually *is* true at the moment. For Evangeline, this was one of them. But that was beside the point. Afraid or not, she certainly wasn't going to allow spiders, spitting, burping, or any other kind, to prevent her from going to the Ikkinasti Jungle with Merriweather and Magdalena.

"If a spider spits at me," she added, "I'll spit right back."

"My dear," her father said, "even if your mother and I thought it was safe enough for you, and even though we want you to experience firsthand the way of the golden-hair, it would still be impossible."

"Nothing's impossible!" announced Evangeline rather more defiantly than she had intended. "At least that's what you always say."

"Yes, but in this case, it *is* impossible, darling," her father continued. "The government of Ikkinasti is giving permission for only *two* people to enter the jungle. They're very fussy about these things, you know. Very sensitive."

So it was settled. Arguing with your parents is one thing, but arguing with an entire government is

another. Don't misunderstand me. You *can* do it. Governments, after all, are made up of people just like you and me, except that most of them carry briefcases and have good teeth. But when you're nine years old, as Evangeline was, it is very difficult.

And so, realizing that when Dr. Aphrodite Pikkaflee calls, primatologists must answer, Evangeline accepted defeat.

But then a new problem occurred to the girl, one that had not yet occurred to her mother and father.

"But if I don't go with you," said Evangeline, looking up at both her parents, "where *am* I going to go?"

Chapter 5

Is She Housebroken?

That question, the one of where Evangeline would stay for the two weeks her parents were in Ikkinasti, was a stumper. Neither Merriweather nor Magdalena had any brothers or sisters, and sadly there were no grandparents left in the family. There was, of course, Magdalena's great-aunt Tizzy. But Tizzy was one hundred and three years old and was convinced that she was the Empress of China.

Try as they might, Merriweather and Magdalena could not think of a suitable place for Evangeline to stay, and for a while it seemed as if their trip to Ikkinasti would have to be canceled. Then, one day, Merriweather was struck by an inspiration.

"I know!" he said to his wife. "I'll write to my

second cousin, twice removed, Melvin. I forgot all about him. I haven't seen him in years, but perhaps Evangeline could stay with him."

In less than a week, Merriweather received a reply from his second cousin, twice removed. Here is what the letter said:

> *Dear Cousin Merriweather,*
>
> *Well, I'll be a monkey's uncle! (Ha! Ha! Get it?) Why anybody in his right mind would want to yuk it up with a bunch of smelly monkeys is more than I can understand, but what the hey! You only live once, right?*
>
> *My wife, India Terpsichore Mudd, and I would be delighted to have Angelica or whatever her name is come and stay with us. We've always been too busy to have a rug rat of our own, but we'd like to know what it would be like to have one around the house.*
>
> *Sincerely,*
> *Melvin*
> *P.S. Is she housebroken? Ha! Ha!*

Evangeline did not consider it an especially good sign that Melvin had written *Angelica* instead of *Evangeline,* but anybody can make a mistake and

Merriweather Mudd had said that his cousin Melvin was a very busy man as the chief executive officer of some kind of business. His wife, if Merriweather remembered correctly, had been a famous ballerina and had traveled the world jumping like a jackrabbit and twirling like a top.

Evangeline was not crazy about the idea of going to stay with Melvin Mudd while her parents were having an adventure in the Ikkinasti Jungle, but she did not mope or whine or pout, as you or I might have.

You see, Evangeline had *spunk*. She was absolutely brimming with the stuff. How did she get it? Perhaps it was because she was born in a garden and her first breath was loaded with the molecules of all living things instead of with the molecules of doctors and nurses and orderlies and antiseptics and weird gasses. Perhaps it was a gift from the butterfly. Perhaps it was just her nature. Who knows? The point is, she had it. And knowing all about the life of the golden-hairs had only strengthened Evangeline's natural mettle. (By the way, if *you* don't have spunk yet, don't worry. There's still time to get it.)

"A golden-hair is ready for anything," her father often said. "They have to be. The jungle is always changing. The golden-hairs who survive are the ones who are able to roll with the punches."

Well, having to stay with her father's second cousin, twice removed, and his wife was certainly a punch. But because Evangeline was who she was, she faced it bravely.

I guess I'll have to roll with it, she told herself. *And who knows? Maybe I'll have a little adventure of my own.*

In preparation for her stay with her father's second cousin, twice removed, Evangeline wrote Melvin and his wife a little note.

> *Dear Cousin Melvin,*
>
> *Thank you very much for letting me come to stay with you. I promise that I will not be any trouble.*
>
> *Please send my regards to your wife, India Terpsichore. Also, my name is Evangeline, not Angelica.*
>
> *Thank you very much.*
>
> *Sincerely,*
>
> *Evangeline Mudd*
>
> *P.S. I like to brachiate. Do you?*

Evangeline wasn't so sure about the "send my regards" part. It sounded too much like a grownup, but she wanted to include her cousin's wife and that was how Magdalena had told her to do it. Also, she had had a great deal of trouble spelling *Terpsichore,* even though she was copying it from Melvin's letter. In the end, though, she was satisfied with her note and mailed it herself.

Time is a funny thing. It's like a soldier that never stops marching. Even though you do everything you can to get him to sit down and take a rest, he won't, which is just one way of saying that all too soon, the day arrived when Evangeline and her parents had to part.

Now, the first time a golden-hair leaves its parents for a little foray into the jungle, there is no folderol. One day, while its mother isn't looking, it just slips away and that's that. It might come back in one week. It might come back in three weeks. It might never come back at all. No one gives it a second thought. But in this regard, the Mudds couldn't have been more human.

When the moment came for Evangeline to board the airplane to her father's second cousin, twice removed (all by herself with the help of a very kindhearted flight attendant, which her parents had paid extra for), there were three very sad and teary Mudds hugging and rubbing noses in the airport.

Evangeline couldn't disguise the two tears that had escaped and were rolling down her cheeks. Her parents were crying, too. (Crying, by the way, has

nothing to do with spunkiness, and don't ever let anybody tell you that it does. Some of the spunkiest people I know cry like a baby at the drop of a hat.)

"We love you," her parents called out to her as she took the flight attendant's hand and walked down the runway toward the door of the plane. "We love you more than anything!"

"I know," she answered. "I love you, too." She looked back over her shoulder one final time. "Be careful!" she cried. "Watch out for the little wormy things and the mosquitoes and . . . the spiders."

"Don't worry about *us*," she heard them reply. "We'll be just fine."

It's only two weeks, she told herself as she settled into her seat in the plane. *Not very much can happen in two weeks.*

You mustn't blame Evangeline for thinking such a

foolish thing. After all, it is probably quite true that in the life of a golden-haired ape, not very much *does* happen in two weeks. But in human life, well, almost anything can happen and usually does.

Chapter 6

MUDD'S MINKS STINK!

It is difficult to say now if Evangeline was lucky or unlucky. It was unlucky that she had been unable to accompany her parents to Ikkinasti. But it was lucky that she had a place to stay with her father's second cousin, twice removed, and his wife. It was lucky that Melvin and India Terpsichore were very rich and could buy Evangeline anything she wanted. But it was unlucky that the only thing she wanted was to see her parents again. It was lucky that Melvin and India Terpsichore allowed Evangeline her independence. It was unlucky that they were such horrid people.

Melvin Mudd was the founder and chief executive officer of Mudd's Marvelous Minks. He was busy night and day turning minks into coats for rich ladies and gentlemen who paid him a great deal of money to do so. Lately, he had been even busier than usual because of "the animal nuts," a group of people who were doing everything they could to force him to shut down his mink farm.

The animal nuts were actually members of an international organization called Pals United for Furry Friends, or PUFFF. They believed that minks had a right to live a life of freedom doing whatever it is that minks like to do without the fear of being turned into a jacket by people like Melvin Mudd. They believed this so strongly that on the day Evangeline arrived they were marching up and down outside Mudd's Manor, the enormous mansion that Melvin Mudd had built for himself and India Terpsichore. There were three of them and all three carried signs that said things like MUDD'S MINKS STINK! and DON'T BE A FINK! STOP MUDD'S MINKS! Lately, they had even started calling the house to ask Melvin Mudd how *he* would like to be turned into a coat.

That first day, Evangeline had asked Melvin why the animal nuts were picketing the house.

"You don't know anything, do you, Angelica?" Melvin snorted, poking Evangeline in the shoulder with a short pudgy finger. "Imagine that *you* are a mink."

This wasn't as easy as it sounded. She had never actually seen a mink. Besides that, what she felt like doing was giving Melvin a poke of his own. But knowing that this was her first day at Mudd's Manor, she shut her eyes and did what she could.

"Imagine," Melvin repeated, "you are a mink on a day when it's hot enough to cook bacon on a beach ball. It's boiling outside! Burning! Broiling! Blistering! Baking! But *you*? *You* are trapped from top to bottom in a mink coat! Wouldn't you hate it? Wouldn't you feel as if you would do anything to get out of that coat?"

Yes, Evangeline said, she guessed she would.

"Of course you would, Evalina," her father's second cousin, twice removed, grunted. "So do the minks. It's torture for them!"

He stopped to light a fancy cigar.

"And that's where I come in, Juanita. I *shave* the minks!"

"You *what?*" Evangeline asked, opening her eyes.

"You heard me! I shave them! I shave them all! Mommy minks. Daddy minks. Baby minks. Even second cousin, twice removed, minks! In return, they give me all that hot, nasty hair. I make it into coats. The minks love it. I love it. And the rich ladies and gentlemen who get to wear those nice warm mink coats love it, too."

Evangeline didn't like the way Melvin rolled his eyes and looked up at the ceiling when he told her that he shaved the minks.

"You see," he concluded. "I am *helping* the minks. In fact, now that I think of it, I am actually a *humanitarian.*"

Evangeline wasn't quite sure what a humanitarian was. Whatever it was, it sounded a lot better than the things the animal nuts were shouting about him from their picket line.

"But if you are helping the minks," she asked, "why are the animal nuts marching up and down in front of your house?"

"What a dummy!" Melvin barked. "They're *jealous*. They'd like to be humanitarians, too, but they can't on account of they don't have any minks of their own."

Evangeline didn't believe this for a second. Maybe she was only nine years old, but she knew what Melvin was doing to turn those minks into coats and it wasn't *shaving* them.

I don't blame the animal nuts for carrying those signs, she thought. *If I could, I would do it, too.*

Things were no better with Melvin's wife, India Terpsichore. Evangeline's father was right. India Terpsichore had been a famous ballerina. She had stopped dancing years ago, but she was positively determined not to let herself go, which meant that she expected at the age of forty to look exactly the way she had looked at the age of sixteen.

India Terpsichore lived in terror of letting herself go. A gray hair sent her immediately to bed and a new wrinkle caused sulking fits that lasted for weeks at a time. She spent hours in front of the huge mirrors staring at herself as she squatted and leaped and spun like a dervish in the dancing studio Melvin had built for her in one wing of Mudd's Manor.

"Others can let themselves go," she would shout as she whizzed about the room, "but not me! Not India Terpsichore Mudd!"

Well, once a prima ballerina, always a prima ballerina.

On Evangeline's first morning at Mudd's Manor, no one bothered to prepare her breakfast or even to ask her how she had slept. Melvin ran out of the house muttering something about the animal nuts. India Terpsichore didn't show her face until after ten o'clock. By that time, Evangeline was so hungry that she had helped herself to what she could find in the kitchen, which amounted to powdered milk and oat flakes.

Evangeline was just taking her first bite when India Terpsichore came leaping into the kitchen in a way that suggested that her front half was doing everything it could to get away from her back half. Evangeline very nearly spilled her entire bowl of cereal onto the floor.

The woman was wearing a pale pink tutu, a pink-and-white striped leotard, and matching pink toe shoes. In her hair, which was pulled back so tightly that Evangeline wondered how she could open and shut her eyes, she had stuck a bunch of pink flowers, which drooped over her face like bait in front of a trout.

"I hope you don't mind," Evangeline managed to say at last. "I helped myself to breakfast."

India Terpsichore didn't seem to hear what Evangeline said, or if she did, she ignored it. Instead, she threw one foot up on the table about six inches from Evangeline's bowl. While Evangeline's eyes grew larger and larger, India Terpsichore began to flex and release the muscles in her foot, which more and more was looking to Evangeline like some alien creature trying to slink its way into her cereal. Next, India Terpsichore began to bend and twist and corkscrew her waist in the way you see ballerinas doing at the barre. One skinny hand was stuck out from her side about six inches from her body; the other was hanging over her head like a dying tulip.

"How do I look today, Evangeleeeen?" she purred.

This question put the girl in a terrible fix. If she told India Terpsichore how she really looked, she would certainly start out poorly with her cousin's wife. On the other hand, she couldn't bring herself to say what she knew India Terpsichore wanted to hear. In the end, the ballerina solved the problem for her, because before the girl could formulate an answer that would be both honest and polite, India Terpsichore answered the question herself.

"Don't tell me!" she hissed. "I already know. Fabulous! I look fabulous, Evangeleeeen."

"Excuse me," the girl said, "but it's Evangeline. The last syllable rhymes with *fine,* not with *mean.* Evangeline."

"Yes, of course," India Terpsichore groaned as she twisted and bounced. "Of course, Evangeleeeen."

Should I? Evangeline thought. *Should I correct her again?*

But before she came to a decision, India Terpsichore flung her foot off the table and began to prance about the perimeter of the kitchen, swishing both arms in crazy half circles in front of her.

"Look at me!" India Terpsichore shouted. "Look at me! I'll bet you can't do this. You've probably let yourself go. That's why!"

And with that, she threw one leg over her head and

twirled like a top. When she stopped twirling, she was planning to ask Evangeline what she thought of *that*, but by the time the room stopped spinning, the chair at the table was empty.

"The little brat," muttered India Terpsichore. "I was just about to perform *Swan Lake* for her, too!"

Chapter 7

Fanning Pink Underwear

The next few days were absolute torture. In the first place, no one at Mudd's Manor paid Evangeline the slightest bit of attention. She fixed all her own meals, and only saw India Terpsichore in the mornings at the breakfast table, where the horrid woman would inch her foot closer and closer to Evangeline's cereal. The rest of the day the ballerina spent in her studio, working like crazy at not letting herself go.

To make matters worse, when Melvin Mudd wasn't raving about the animal nuts, who continued, Evangeline noticed, to appear in front of Mudd's Manor, he was "bouncing ideas off her."

"Hey, you!" he would roar, bounding through the doors of Mudd's Manor. "Hey, Esmerelda! Come here! I have some new ideas I want to bounce off you."

As chief executive officer of an important company, Melvin Mudd never merely explained his ideas; he always *bounced them off* someone.

Evangeline was perplexed as to why he had chosen *her*. She knew nothing about turning minks into coats for rich ladies and gentlemen, and what's more, she didn't want to know anything about such a horrible business. But almost from the very first day she had arrived, Melvin had sought her out for this purpose. It was practically the only time he talked to her.

"Mink underwear!" he would bellow as he paced up and down, puffing on a cigar. "Mink underwear made from baby minks. Whaddya think?" Or "Mink bathing trunks! Just think of it, Angelina. Mink bathing trunks! Mink bikinis, too! Rich ladies and gentlemen like to swim just like everybody else. They have a right. They deserve it. Whaddya think?"

Evangeline remained silent when Melvin presented these ideas to her. She knew very well that anyone who spent his life thinking about bopping baby minks on the head so that he could turn them into underwear for rich ladies and gentlemen should not be trusted. If she had said anything, she would have

told him that they were beastly ideas, as beastly as Melvin himself. Anyway, it didn't really make any difference because Melvin didn't actually want her to respond. He was merely bouncing ideas off her, as though she were a brick wall and he were a playground bully with a big rubber ball.

But, like all bullies, Melvin was filled with fear. It was the animal nuts. He was terrified that they would somehow find out about his new ideas and prevent him from making them real.

"They don't even like mink *coats*," he would whine. "What would they say about mink underwear!"

It was after one of these sessions that Evangeline went up to her room to look at the calendar she had brought with her.

Only ten more days, she told herself as she counted the *X*'s she had drawn through the days she had been at Mudd's Manor. *Only ten more days.*

It was a breezy summer afternoon, and a branch from one of the large maple trees that grew around the house and lined the walk to the street was tapping against her windowpane. *Tap-tap! Tap-tap! Tap-tap!* It was almost as if the branch were tapping Evangeline herself.

Come on! it seemed to say. *Have some fun!*

She went to the window.

Why didn't I think of it before? she asked herself.

And with that, she opened the sash, grabbed the branch that had been tapping against it, and before you could say mink underwear, was swinging through the treetops as if she had been born in Mudd's Manor and had done it every day of her life. The foliage was so lush that she realized she could brachiate in perfect secrecy. Not a soul could see her.

It took her no time at all to learn her way around. Soon, she made her way out to the trees growing over the sidewalk where the animal nuts were picketing. She stopped on a branch directly above them to get a better look.

One was very tall and very thin and wore a bright yellow dress. She reminded Evangeline of a number-two pencil. Another was a little round bald man whose pink skin and pink scalp put Evangeline in mind of an eraser, and not a new eraser either, but one of those that has spent its life rubbing out other people's mistakes. The third animal nut, whom Evangeline immediately nicknamed the Smudge, was the messiest person she had ever seen, so messy in fact that Evangeline wasn't quite sure if the Smudge was a man animal nut or a woman animal nut.

"Mudd's minks stink," they were chanting. "Mudd's minks stink!"

Evangeline's intention had been to study the animal nuts. She wanted to get a better look at the people who Melvin said were "jealous" of him. But almost before she knew what she was doing, she called out to them.

"*Psssst. Psssst.* I'm up here!"

The Pencil saw her first, then the Eraser, and finally the Smudge, who was so surprised to see a girl sitting in the trees that he—for Evangeline had decided that it *was* a he—tripped on his shoelace and went sprawling.

"He's planning mink underwear!" Evangeline whispered as loudly as she could.

"What?" said the Pencil. "He's fanning pink underwear? Who? Why would anybody in his right mind fan pink underwear?"

"I don't believe it!" the Eraser proclaimed, his face turning even pinker with anger. "He ought to be arrested!"

"It's horrible!" the Smudge cried out in a voice that made Evangeline feel that the Smudge was a woman after all. "Horrible!"

"Not *pink* underwear! *Mink* underwear!" whispered Evangeline. "Cousin Melvin. He's planning to make mink underwear."

Fearful that she might be drawing attention to herself from the house, she took off and brachiated her way back to her room.

That afternoon, Melvin came home to new signs. DOWN WITH MINK UNDERWEAR! and WE CAUGHT MUDD WITH HIS PANTS DOWN! IT'S NOT A PRETTY SIGHT! MINK UNDERWEAR? NO WAY!

He was furious.

"How could they know?" he shrieked. The cigar smoke billowed around him. It was as if his brain were on fire. "There must be a spy at the ranch. I'll have to give up! I'll have to go with the mink bathing trunks."

The next morning Evangeline swung out to the animal nuts.

"Now it's bathing trunks," she whispered. "Mink bathing trunks."

"YOU'LL SINK IN MUDD'S MINK!" the animal nuts chanted as Melvin got out of his car that afternoon.

"They've bugged the phones!" he howled. "Be careful what you say, Lavinia! They've probably got microphones everywhere!"

And he ripped off his jacket to see if someone had sewn a tiny microphone where a button should be.

It never occurred to him that Evangeline was the spy. He simply could not conceive that a rug rat could be so clever.

But she was. And as the days went by, Melvin Mudd was not the only resident of Mudd's Manor to be taken in by Evangeline's cleverness.

Chapter 8
Play! Play! Play!

Evangeline happened on the piano in one of the endless rooms that made up the hideous house. It was her third day at Mudd's Manor.

"It's horribly out of tune," she said aloud as she ran her fingers up and down the keys, "but it's better than nothing."

For the next two afternoons, while Melvin was at the mink ranch and India Terpsichore was in her dancing studio, Evangeline came to the room and played all the songs she had learned with Madame Valentina Kloudishkaya. She had played these songs, too, during the evenings at the cozy bungalow with Merriweather and Magdalena, and the music took her back to those happy times. But on the third afternoon, India Terpsichore swept into the room like a dancing banshee.

"Evangeleeeen!" she shrieked. "You sly creature! Why didn't you tell me you played the piano?"

Before Evangeline could say a word, India Terpsichore had her by the wrist and was dragging her out of the room.

"Come with me!" she ordered, though Evangeline thought it was unnecessary to say anything at all since her hold on the girl's wrist was tighter than a boa constrictor's.

India Terpsichore pulled Evangeline down a series of long, dark halls until, eventually, they arrived at a set of large double doors. These the woman shoved open with a flourish of one long, skinny hand. With the other, she yanked Evangeline into a dancing studio that was practically the size of a gymnasium. The walls were lined with mirrors. It was entirely empty except for a dilapidated grand piano standing like a lonely watchdog in one corner.

The ballerina shoved Evangeline down onto the piano's bench and took off around the perimeter of the room, leaping like a monkey with ants in its pants.

"Now play!" she commanded. "Play while I dance!

Play Bach! Play Bartók! Play Bazzini! Play anything you like, you little fool, but play! Play! Play!"

That afternoon, and all the afternoons that followed, India Terpsichore found Evangeline and forced her to play the piano while she cavorted around the room.

Often she would order Evangeline to watch her perform a particular step.

"This is what I did when I danced for the Duke and Duchess of Snervlakia," she would hoot. "They thought I was fantastic! They thought I was terrific! They thought I was maaaarvelous!"

Then she would twirl violently until there was nothing left of her but a pasty, spinning blur.

To make matters worse, if Evangeline tried to take a break in order to rest her aching hands and arms, India Terpsichore would come whirling over to the piano like a pink tornado.

"Why are you stopping?" she would pant, perspiration dripping off her like she had been standing in a downpour. "Don't stop! Don't ever stop!"

On the day India Terpsichore realized that Evangeline could play almost anything, she began to make even more specific demands. That was the day Evangeline decided to take matters into her own hands, tired as they were.

It was the third afternoon of Evangeline's enforced accompanying. She had been playing for two hours straight when India Terpsichore came prancing up to the piano like a circus pony.

"Play the rondo from Beethoven's Ninth," India Terpsichore ordered one afternoon. "I want to practice my *ciseaux*."

Now, in case you don't know it, the *ciseaux* (that's French, by the way—almost all ballet terms are, you know) is a dance step in which the ballerina jumps straight up in the air like a rocket and opens and closes her legs as many times as she can like a pair of deranged scissors. (It's not that easy, and if you don't believe me, you should stop reading and get up and try it.)

India Terpsichore was obsessed with the *ciseaux*. It had been her specialty, and in her younger days she could cut the air like crazy, *ciseaux*ing all over the place.

Before she began, she clapped her bony hands together, beating out the time for Evangeline.

"One. Two. Thrrrree. Four," she counted majestically. "One. Two. Thrrrree. Four."

Evangeline's own sense of rhythm and musical time were perfect, far better than India Terpsichore's, and the last thing she needed was for the ballerina to tell her how to play the rondo from Beethoven's

Ninth. Why, it was practically the first thing she had learned. But as she sat at the piano, Evangeline was struck with an inspiration.

"One. Two. Thrrrree. Four," the girl said, counting along with India Terpsichore and rolling her *r*'s just the way the ridiculous woman had. "One. Two. Thrrrree. Four."

As she counted, she began to play the rondo. India Terpsichore spun away from the piano to the middle of the room, where she began to *ciseaux* in time with the music.

"Look at me!" she shouted. "Just look at me! Others have let themselves go. But not me! Not India Terpsichore Mudd!"

It was at that point that Evangeline began to speed the music up. India Terpsichore didn't notice, of course. She was only interested in herself and her *ciseaux,* so before she knew it, Evangeline had her jumping up and down faster than a jackhammer and *ciseaux*ing like crazy. Then, just at the point when it seemed impossible for the woman to *ciseaux* one more time, Evangeline slowed the music down, slower and s-l-o-w-e-r and s—l—o—w—e—r and s——l——o——w——e——r.

Now, you should know by now how hard it is to *ciseaux* even when the music is playing at the speed it's supposed to, so you can imagine how hard it is to do in slow motion. It just can't be done.

"I don't understand it!" India Terpsichore wailed. "What's happened to my *ciseaux*?"

"Perhaps . . . ," Evangeline suggested slyly. "Perhaps, Cousin India Terpsichore, you . . . you have let yourself go."

This sent the woman into such a fit that the dancing stopped altogether and Evangeline got the afternoon off.

And so, one by one, the days passed at Mudd's Manor. Evangeline spent her mornings brachiating and informing the animal nuts of Melvin's latest plans. She spent her afternoons alternately speeding up and slowing down India Terpsichore's music until the woman didn't know if she was jitterbugging or waltzing.

The evenings Evangeline reserved for herself and thinking of her beloved parents, remembering the happy times they had had in the past and planning for more happy times in the future.

I can do this, she would tell herself each night. *It's only two weeks. I can do this.* Finally, there were fourteen *X*'s on Evangeline's calendar. The day had arrived for her parents to pick her up.

Though they weren't expected at Mudd's Manor until six o'clock in the evening, Evangeline packed her bags first thing in the morning. By five that afternoon, she was sitting on the doorstep waiting. By seven, she was puzzled. *They must have missed a bus,* she told herself. By eight, she was angry. *Why don't they call? It's very inconsiderate.* By nine, she was worried. *Where can they be?* And by ten, she was downright frantic. *I hope it wasn't the spiders. Oh, I hope it wasn't that!*

The next morning Melvin found Evangeline asleep on the doorstep. She had waited throughout the night.

"Emmelina!" the CEO said, nudging her with the toe of his heavy black shoe. "Emmelina! Wake up!"

Evangeline opened her eyes and smiled. She had been having a lovely dream. She and Merriweather and Magdalena were back at the cozy bungalow. They were sitting in the garden, and the lilies and the roses and heliotropes were all abloom, just as her mother had told her they were on the day she was born.

But slowly, as the girl became more and more awake, her dream faded and the horrible truth began to dawn on her. Her parents had never arrived. She was still at Mudd's Manor.

"Wake up, Emmelina!" Melvin boomed. "Wake up! I have some ideas I want to bounce off you."

Chapter 9

Wish You Were Here

Curiously, neither Melvin Mudd nor his wife, India Terpsichore, acknowledged that Evangeline's parents were missing, and when she tried to bring the subject up to Melvin, she got nowhere.

"Excuse me, sir," she had begun.

(Just as Melvin never knew what to call Evangeline, Evangeline was never certain how to address her father's second cousin, twice removed. Somehow she couldn't bring herself to call him Melvin. *Mr.* Mudd, on the other hand, reminded her of her father, and the chief executive officer was nothing like her beloved father, nothing at all. Out of desperation, she finally settled on calling him sir.)

"Excuse me, sir," she had begun. "But as you know, my parents left for the jungles of the Ikkinasti rain forest and . . ."

"Jungle, did you say?" Melvin had shouted, interrupting her. "Rain forest? What a fantastic idea I've just had, Esmelvina. I'm going to bounce it off you right now. Are you ready? I hope so, because here it comes! Jungle hats! Mink jungle hats! Rich ladies and gentlemen occasionally go on safari. They need to look stylish. Whaddya think?"

Worse, when Evangeline brought the subject up to India Terpsichore, she was met with a scolding.

"What are you so poopy-faced about?" the horrid woman had said. "Most girls your age would love to have a second cousin, twice removed, with a wife who was not letting herself go."

Day after dreary day passed. Days turned to weeks, weeks turned to months, and still there was no sign of Merriweather or Magdalena. Evangeline was beside herself with grief and worry.

Where could they be? she thought over and over. *Where could they be?*

But as upset as she was, she also tried to remember everything her parents had taught her.

"When a golden-hair is in a situation it cannot do anything about," they had often said, "it walks away and does something else. You see, darling, it knows that eventually the first situation will take care of itself in one way or another."

Evangeline wasn't so sure about the "one way or another" part, because the only way that *this* situation could take care of itself would be to end by uniting her with her parents. But because it was not her nature to dwell on such things, she did what she could to follow her parents' advice and get busy with the something elses.

The first something else she did was to write a letter to Dr. Aphrodite Pikkaflee. Here is what the letter said:

> *Dear Dr. Pikkaflee,*
>
> *My name is Evangeline Mudd. My mother and father haven't returned from Ikkinasti and I am worried sick. We've got to do something! Please help me find my parents.*
>
> *Sincerely,*
>
> *Evangeline Mudd*
>
> *P.S. I am staying at Mudd's Manor with my father's second cousin, twice removed, and his wife.*
>
> *P.P.S. It isn't fun.*

Every day after mailing the letter, Evangeline ran to meet the letter carrier to see if a reply had come, but every day it was the same—threatening letters to Melvin Mudd from PUFFF and other organizations like it and piles of beauty magazines for India Terpsichore.

"You should read these, Evangeleeeen," the ballerina once said to the girl. "You look to me like you're letting yourself go."

The second something else was to intensify her campaign against Mudd's Marvelous Minks.

Almost immediately after her parents had disappeared, Evangeline began to have terrible nightmares about the mink ranch. She had never been there, of course, but in her dreams the ranch was a horrible place filled with nothing but cages. Melvin Mudd was there and he was choosing which minks were going to be turned into jackets. The minks were scared and making crying noises almost like human babies. But that wasn't the worst part. The worst part was that *she* was in one of the cages.

It was a morning after one of these dreams that Evangeline made a solemn vow to herself.

"One day, I'll help those minks at Melvin's ranch," she whispered to herself. "I don't know how, and I don't know when, but I will!"

In the meantime, she began to encourage her father's second cousin, twice removed, to bounce ideas off her so that she could report them to the animal nuts.

Though Evangeline was doing what she could to keep her spirits up, the months at Mudd's Manor were lonelier than what any child (or adult, either) should have to put up with. Evangeline's tenth birthday came and went without a single candle.

Her one source of comfort at Mudd's Manor was contained in a little wooden box that she kept by her bedside table. It was a postcard, a postcard she had received from her parents her sixth day at Mudd's Manor. It had been sent from Bababun, a village on the outskirts of the Ikkinasti Jungle and the last place her parents had been seen.

Dear Evangeline,

We love you. Wish you were here. See you soon.
Merry and Magdalena

Evangeline Mudd
c/o Mudd Manor
Wilbur Road

Every morning just after she woke up, and every night just before she went to bed, Evangeline would remove the postcard from its box. The picture side of the postcard showed a mother and father golden-hair with their new baby. On the back of the postcard, almost illegible from tearstains and finger smudges, was the short message her parents had written. At the top, almost completely covered by a stamp, was a cartoon face of a golden-hair drawn in ink by Magdalena.

Now, if it had been you or I reading that postcard, our hearts might have broken. But Evangeline wasn't you and she wasn't me. She was *herself,* and to be yourself is a very powerful thing. In fact, it just might be the most powerful thing a person *can* be. So instead of Evangeline's heart breaking every time she read the postcard, her heart grew stronger.

I was happy once, she would tell herself. *And I'll be happy again. I won't have to stay here forever. Someday, I'll leave Mudd's Manor and when I do, I'll go to Ikkinasti myself and look for my parents.*

Evangeline had no way of knowing that *someday* was just around the corner. It always is, you know.

Chapter 10
Foul Play

One afternoon toward the beginning of her fourth month at Mudd's Manor, Evangeline was sitting at her bedroom window when a small black car stopped in the middle of the street in front of the house.

This, in itself, was nothing unusual. Black cars pulled up in front of the mansion all the time. Melvin Mudd was constantly being visited by the rich ladies and gentlemen who bought his jackets, and their cars always seemed to be black, even the windows. But this car definitely did not belong to one of Melvin Mudd's customers. Melvin's customers drove only the latest models, with telephones and televisions and refrigerators and satellite homing devices and who knows what else. *This* car looked like it had been made before there even *were* telephones!

I said before that the car was black, but that wasn't entirely true because the fender that covered the front tire on the passenger's side was a kind of rust color and the fender that covered the rear tire on the driver's side was bright blue. Smoke was seeping out from under the hood, and every once in a while the car would make a loud popping noise and hop off the ground as if it had a very bad case of the hiccups.

"It must be another animal nut," Evangeline said aloud.

She made this conjecture based upon the car that the Pencil, the Eraser, and the Smudge arrived in each morning. While it was not quite as unusual as the car that had pulled up, it *was* very old, with the antenna for the radio broken off and a wire coat hanger stuck in its place. This car, which her new friends always parked directly in front of Mudd's Manor, drove Melvin crazy. He positively hated that car!

"They're already animal nuts," he would snarl. "Do they have to be car nuts, too?"

Melvin had left early in the day to head out to the mink ranch. India Terpsichore was spending the day, as she sometimes did, at Renaud's Revitalizing Ranch for the Rich and wRinkled.

Evangeline was sorry that Melvin wasn't at home to see this new car, for if the car with the broken antenna drove him crazy, *this one,* the girl thought, *would send him totally around the bend.*

But when the car door opened and Evangeline saw the driver step out, she stopped thinking altogether. She had never seen such a person in all her life. First of all, she, for it was a she, was shorter than Evangeline herself. Second, the driver, who wore a baggy red dress with blue flowers printed on it, was as wide as she was high.

It wouldn't be right though to say she is fat, Evangeline thought. *She looks too strong to be called fat.*

Evangeline remembered a television show she had seen about a family of monkeys who were always getting into all kinds of trouble. The show, which really hadn't been very good, was called *Monkey House,* and in it the monkeys wore human clothes and spoke English. The driver of the black car, Evangeline suddenly realized, reminded her very much of the mother monkey in *Monkey House.* It could only be one person.

"Dr. Pikkaflee!" Evangeline whispered. "Dr. Aphrodite Pikkaflee!"

Evangeline raced down the wide marble hall and on down the long flight of marble stairs that led to the

front entry. Without another thought, she pulled open the heavy oak door to Mudd's Manor.

"Dr. Pikkaflee!" she shouted.

For a moment, Dr. Pikkaflee stopped in her tracks and stared at the girl.

"My dear child," she finally said. "You are a sight for sore eyes!"

Without a word, she trotted up to the girl and wrapped her long arms around her. She patted her back and lifted her enormous hand to Evangeline's scalp to groom it, just the way her mother used to.

For her part, Evangeline hugged Dr. Pikkaflee so tightly that the little woman wondered if Evangeline was ever going to let go.

Dear me, she thought. *It's worse than I had imagined.*

Eventually, Evangeline did let go of Dr. Pikkaflee and led her through the front hall and into the room that India Terpsichore insisted on calling the great room, though Evangeline was always tempted to ask what was so great about it. It was nearly as big as a football field. There were chairs and sofas, of course, but they were so modern in design that it was nearly impossible to know where one was actually meant to sit on them. Dr. Pikkaflee and Evangeline finally settled down on the floor in front of one of the windows.

"Dear me," said Dr. Pikkaflee when Evangeline finished telling her about her life with the Mudds. "Dear, dear me. And what of your parents? Have you heard anything? Anything at all?"

Evangeline held herself steady.

"Nothing," she finally managed to say. "Nothing except a postcard from Bababun."

"I'd like to see that postcard later," said Dr. Pikkaflee. "In the meantime, my dear, there are some things I must share with you."

Evangeline listened as Dr. Pikkaflee went on to

explain that, amazingly, she had just learned of Merriweather and Magdalena's disappearance.

"It was my own stubborn nature that did it," she said in her strange, soft accent, an accent that Evangeline could not place, try as she might. The only thing she knew for certain is that it wasn't one of the familiar ones, French or German or Spanish.

"Even though my leg was broken, I decided to continue my experiment of living in the treetops. I figured that occasionally a golden-hair must hurt herself, and I thought it might be useful to see how one would maneuver with a broken leg. I thought perhaps that I could contribute something new to the field of science, don't you see?

"Unfortunately, I wasn't quite up to it. I fell again. On my head. I was unconscious for three and a half weeks. When I woke up, I believed that I was a capuchin monkey. I believed that until yesterday! I am fortunate in that I have some very good friends who saw me through it."

Evangeline remarked how dreadful it must be to believe you are a capuchin monkey. "Almost as awful," she said, "as living with Melvin and India Terpsichore Mudd."

"Oh, it wasn't nearly as bad as *that*," Dr. Pikkaflee

replied. "I ate nothing but bananas, of course. A wonderful diet, I must say. I'm as strong as an ox now. My only regret is that I didn't write anything down. I mean my thoughts as a capuchin monkey. They would have been very interesting, don't you think? But how could I? Capuchin monkeys do not know how to write. And now I can't remember a thing about it. It's as if it never happened."

Evangeline hoped that someday the time at Mudd's Manor would seem as if *it* had never happened.

Still, the girl admitted to herself, *it must be very strange to have spent a great deal of time believing yourself to be a monkey and then not be able to remember anything about it. Perhaps,* she thought later, *it's a good thing. Monkeys do have some rather embarrassing habits.*

"I suddenly came out of it," Dr. Pikkaflee continued. "That was just yesterday. The first thing I did after reading your letter was to come and find you. I feel responsible, don't you see? After all, I was the one who asked them to go to the tropical rain forest of Ikkinasti. It's all my fault."

For a moment neither Evangeline nor Dr. Pikkaflee spoke. Dr. Pikkaflee was perhaps waiting for the girl to agree with her, to say that yes it *was* all her fault. But it never occurred to Evangeline to think such a thing.

"I . . . I haven't told you everything," Aphrodite

Pikkaflee resumed as soon as she realized that Evangeline was not going to blame her for what had happened.

It seemed to Evangeline that Dr. Aphrodite Pikkaflee had suddenly become uncertain of what she was going to say next. She pulled at her ear. She scratched the top of her head. She groomed herself and looked out the window.

"I have reason to believe," she finally continued, "that there may have been some *foul play.*"

Evangeline wasn't absolutely sure that she knew what *foul play* meant. The only thing she knew for certain was that it almost always involved trouble.

"Foul play?" she asked. "What do you mean?"

"That's what I intend to find out," Dr. Aphrodite Pikkaflee responded. "By going to the rain forest of Ikkinasti myself!"

Evangeline jumped up from the floor. "You mean you're going to look for them?" she shouted.

"That's exactly what I mean," Dr. Pikkaflee answered, standing up herself.

Before Dr. Pikkaflee could say another word, Evangeline left the good doctor standing in the living room and ran toward the stairs.

"Where are you going, child?" Dr. Pikkaflee called out after her.

"To get my things," Evangeline answered. "I'm coming with you!"

"But, my dear child," said Dr. Pikkaflee with a worried furrow of her brow, "the jungle is a dangerous place. It's full of—"

"I know all about the little wormy things and the mosquitoes," the girl said, a little more loudly than she had meant to.

She knew it was very rude to interrupt, and as a rule tried never to do it, but there are times when a person's feelings are more important than good manners. (Please don't tell your parents I said that, but it happens to be true.)

"I even know about the spiders," she continued, a little softer now. "But I don't care about them. Any of them. The only thing I care about is finding my parents."

For a moment Aphrodite Pikkaflee said nothing. She simply looked at Evangeline with her large brown eyes. Evangeline had the uncomfortable feeling that she was being studied.

"Well," Dr. Pikkaflee finally remarked, scratching her ear, "the government of Ikkinasti *did* give me *two* permits to enter the jungle."

Chapter 11

Biddly-poo-pa—?

Evangeline threw her few things into her bag. Nothing was going to stop her now.

"This time," she said aloud to no one in particular, "I'll take on the whole government of Ikkinasti if I have to. I am going to that jungle and I am going to find my parents!"

She looked out the window of her room one final time. The animal nuts were calling it quits for the day, packing their signs into the car with the coat hanger for the antenna. In a matter of seconds Evangeline was brachiating out to the sidewalk as she had done almost every day for nearly four months.

"I'm leaving," she called down to the Pencil when

she got to the branch that hung above the car. "I'm leaving to find my parents, but I'll be back one day. To rescue the minks. I promise."

"Bless you, child!" the Pencil called out. "Bless you. And good luck!"

But Evangeline hadn't heard. She was already flying through the trees on her way back.

Minutes later she was nestled safely in the front seat of the little black car with Dr. Aphrodite Pikkaflee stepping on the gas. Each passing second left Mudd's Manor farther and farther behind.

Evangeline hadn't waited for Melvin or India Terpsichore's return. She had simply left a note to her father's second cousin, twice removed, and his wife. The note consisted of two words. *I'm leaving.* She hadn't even signed her name.

"Why should I?" she had said to Dr. Pikkaflee. "Melvin never bothered to learn it, and India Terpsichore mispronounced it."

"Quite right!" Dr. Pikkaflee had said. "Quite right!"

The little black car was zooming down the road. To Evangeline, it seemed that the car knew the way all by itself, like a horse finding its way to the barn.

"Before we leave for Ikkinasti, there are one or two things we have to do," Dr. Aphrodite Pikkaflee shouted.

Dr. Pikkaflee had to shout because of the racket that was emanating from under the hood of the car. It roared. It rattled. It squealed. It squeaked! And every once in a while, it emitted a noise that can only be described as a burp! To Evangeline the racket was sweeter than music. It was the noise of adventure. It was the noise of finding her parents.

"What kind of things?" Evangeline shouted back to Dr. Pikkaflee.

"Oh, nothing serious," yelled Dr. Pikkaflee. "Just your . . ."

At that moment, the car let out a tremendous bang so that Evangeline couldn't be sure what the doctor had said. But it almost sounded like she had said "injections." "Nothing serious. Just your injections."

Now, Evangeline knew that *injections* was a fancy word for shots, the kind a doctor gives you with long, pointy needles.

Perhaps she said infections, Evangeline told herself. *Nothing serious. Just your infections.* The trouble was, Evangeline didn't have any infections that she knew of. She had scraped her knee the day before, sliding down the banister at Mudd's Manor, but the tiny red mark it left could hardly be described as an infection.

"You can't go into the tropical rain forest of

Ikkinasti without injections, Evangeline, dear," Dr. Pikkaflee shouted, popping a banana into her mouth. "It's too dangerous, what with the little wormy things and the huge mosquitoes and all."

"How many injections will I have to get?" Evangeline asked.

"Oh, not many," Dr. Pikkaflee answered cheerfully. "Only about twenty or thirty. Banana, my dear?"

Twenty or thirty? Evangeline simply couldn't imagine where she was going to get twenty or thirty shots, and when she asked, Dr. Pikkaflee's answer was not reassuring.

"In your arm, of course," she said, "and elsewhere."

Later that afternoon, it was a very uncomfortable Evangeline Mudd who found herself sitting next to Dr. Aphrodite Pikkaflee in a small, tidy waiting room with ALPHONSO OUCH, M.D., printed on its door.

Evangeline was trying to remember what *M.D.* stood for when the door to the examination room swung open.

"Aphrodite Pikkaflee!" exclaimed a tiny man with tufts of white hair sprouting from his head, his eyebrows, and even his ears! It looked to Evangeline like a cloud had settled over him, taking root wherever it found a promising spot.

"Dr. Alphonso Ouch, permit me to introduce Miss Evangeline Mudd," said Dr. Pikkaflee rather formally. "She and I are about to undertake an adventure in the tropical rain forest of Ikkinasti."

"Ikkinasti, you say?" asked Dr. Ouch gravely, as he twisted the hair in both ears into fine, soft points. "I see."

He bent down to get a closer look at Evangeline, producing a wide popsicle stick from the pocket of his white doctor's tunic as he did so.

"Open your mouth and say *ah*," he said.

Evangeline wondered why doctors always felt they had to tell you to open your mouth to say *ah* since no one she knew could say *ah* without doing it, but she did as she was asked.

"Ahhhhh."

"Again," Dr. Ouch ordered. He began to poke around Evangeline's mouth with the flat stick.

"Ahhhhh."

Is it my imagination, thought Evangeline, *or does that stick taste like chocolate?*

"Now say *oooooooooooooh!*" Dr. Ouch instructed.

"Ooooooooooooooh!" said the girl. The flavor of the stick was changing from chocolate to orange.

"Eeeeeeeeeeeeeeeeeeee."

"Eeeeeeeeeeeeeeeeee," she repeated. The stick went from orange to mint. It was unbelievably yummy!

"Babaa-ba-ree-bop!" shouted the doctor.

"Babaa-ba-ree-bop!" Evangeline shouted back. She was willing to say whatever Dr. Ouch asked as long as that popsicle stick kept producing flavors. It was now cherry, by the way.

"Ramalamadingdong!"

"Ramalamadingdong!"

Lime.

"Itchy-witchy-booboo-scattywattydoo!"

"Itchy-witchy-booboo-scattywattydoo!"

Vanilla.

"Biddly-poo-pa—" Dr. Ouch broke off mid-syllable and stood up, taking the delicious stick, which was just hinting at pistachio, with him. "That's all!" he said. "Good luck. Farewell. Bye bye."

"But . . . ," said Evangeline, doing what she could to hold on to the pistachio flavor that was rapidly fading from her tongue. "But . . . ?"

"But what?" said the doctor, twirling his eyebrows.

"But what about the shots?"

"Oh, *those*." Dr. Ouch replied in a tone of voice that suggested that he really shouldn't have to explain such a thing. "I gave them to you already. One hand was holding the stick. What did you think the other hand was doing?"

"You gave me all of them?" Evangeline asked. "Including the one for the little wormy things?"

Dr. Ouch nodded.

Evangeline was amazed. She had had twenty or thirty shots in her arm and elsewhere and hadn't even known it. She wondered how Dr. Ouch had even gotten to her elsewhere since she was sitting on it during the examination, but she decided not to bring it up. She did have one question, though.

"Excuse me, Dr. Ouch," she said.

The doctor responded by untwirling his ear tufts.

"Did you also give me a shot for the spitting spiders? The ones that cause you to, well . . . you know."

Dr. Ouch looked at Evangeline as if he hadn't quite understood her.

"Didn't you tell her, Aphrodite?" he asked.

Dr. Pikkaflee suddenly took an interest in what was happening out the window, which was, as far as Evangeline could tell, exactly nothing.

"There is no vaccine for the spiders," Dr. Ouch finally said. "If you run into one of those spitting spiders, you've had it!"

Chapter 12

Shivers and Shakes

"We'll spend the night at my house and leave for Ikkinasti first thing tomorrow morning," said Dr. Pikkaflee as the two got back into the little black car. "I hope you don't have acrophobia, my dear."

Evangeline wasn't sure what acrophobia was. Whatever it was, she hoped it didn't require another injection.

"You mean where your mouth gets all foamy and you run around in circles and try to bite people?" she asked.

She tried hard to recall the last time she had bitten someone. Luckily, she couldn't recall a single time.

"You are thinking of *hydrophobia*, my dear," said

Dr. Pikkaflee. "*Acrophobia* is completely different. *Acrophobia* is a fear of high places. I live in a tree house, you know."

And what a tree house it was! Evangeline had never seen anything like it. Built not in one tree, but in a group of three ancient beeches that looked as if they had grown together since the beginning of time, Dr. Pikkaflee's house was a fantastic combination of architecture and nature. Each room was on a different level and was connected to the others by a series of walkways and narrow winding steps. But Evangeline soon discovered that you could also get from room to room by swinging on the countless ropes that Dr. Pikkaflee had placed strategically in the trees.

"You certainly are your parents' daughter," marveled Dr. Pikkaflee. "I've never seen a human brachiate quite so well."

Evangeline grabbed the rope that dangled in front of her and did a double flip.

She went to bed early that night, though I suppose I should say that she went "to hammock," because that, in fact, was what she was sleeping in. The hammock, which was woven from twine, was tied at one end to a support built especially for it and at the other end to a large branch that intersected the room.

"Rest well," Dr. Pikkaflee had said as she rubbed

noses with the girl and gently rocked the hammock. "Tomorrow is a big day."

But before Dr. Pikaflee had finished her sentence, Evangeline was already asleep. For the first night in weeks, she didn't dream she was in a cage at Melvin Mudd's mink ranch.

When she awoke the next morning, the sun was already shining, dappling her room in a marvelous display of shadow and light. She could hear the trills and songs of hundreds of birds.

"Today!" the birds seemed to be singing. "Today is *someday!*"

Now, those of you have spent time in a hammock know that a hammock and a bed have nothing whatever in common. No, a hammock and a bed are as different from each other as your cranky uncle Morton is from your naughty cousin Eddie, for a bed is a stodgy old thing with all four feet on the floor while a hammock is a free spirit known the world over as a practical joker.

That is why, when Evangeline swung her legs over the side of the hammock just the way she would have done if she had been in her bed at Mudd's Manor, she found herself sprawled face-down on the floor with the hammock swinging merrily above. The hammock had tipped her out!

But she didn't care. She didn't care at all.

It was exciting! It was exciting to wake up in a tree house! It was even exciting to get toppled by a hammock!

So exciting, Evangeline decided, *that I think I'll do it again.*

She was working her way back into the hammock when Dr. Pikkaflee knocked softly on the door.

"Evangeline, dear," she said, "are you awake? Come down for breakfast. The plane is waiting for us."

"The plane?" the girl asked.

"You didn't think we were going to swim to Ikkinasti, did you?" Dr. Pikkaflee chuckled.

Evangeline tried to get both feet on the floor, but before she could, the hammock whirled her around like a jump rope going double dutch. Finally, her head spinning, she threw on her clothes and swung down to the kitchen.

Evangeline hadn't been aware of anyone else's presence in the tree house, which is why it was very surprising when Dr. Pikkaflee stopped cooking breakfast to make a formal introduction.

"Evangeline," she said. "Meet Pansy. Pansy, this is Evangeline."

Evangeline looked across the table, where she had been about to take a seat, to find a young golden-haired ape. The ape appeared to be about six or seven months old, and bore the same quizzical expression that Evangeline had seen so many times in her mother's drawings.

Pansy stood up on the chair in which she had been eating a banana and gave a little bow. Evangeline did the best she could by curtseying.

"Pansy is from Ikkinasti," explained Dr. Pikkaflee. "An orphan. Her parents were . . . well, let's just say that some friends found her starving in the jungle and brought her here."

An immediate tenderness swept over the girl. After all, she was an orphan, too. Kind of, anyway.

"It's very nice to meet you, Pansy," Evangeline said, hoping that this was the proper way to talk to an ape. Pansy pulled out the chair next to hers and, by pointing to it with her lips, indicated to Evangeline that she should sit there.

Throughout breakfast, Evangeline remained silent, eating her banana porridge and listening to the words of the song that Dr. Pikkaflee sang as she puttered about the kitchen.

In old Ikkinasti
I have to admit
The jungles are jumping
With spiders who spit.
They'll find you and blind you
Lickety-split.
Then have you for dinner
Kaboodle and kit.
Oh swing-a-ling, swing-a-ling, swing-a-ling-oh
Swing-a-ling-oh, swing-a-ling-oh
Swing-a-ling, swing-a-ling, swing-a-ling-
ooooooooooooooooh
Let the breezy breezes blow.

In old Ikkinasti,
Mosquitoes and snakes!
They'll give you the quivers
And shivers and shakes.
Your skin will come off
In hideous flakes.
But you'll be all right
If you've got what it takes.
Oh swing-a-ling, swing-a-ling, swing-a-ling-oh
Swing-a-ling-oh, swing-a-ling-oh
Swing-a-ling, swing-a-ling, swing-a-ling-

ooooooooooooooooooh
Let the breezy breezes blow.

By the time the song was done, Pansy had moved over into the girl's lap. But as happy as this made Evangeline, the words to the second verse of the song kept repeating themselves over and over again.

Is it true? she wondered. *Is it true that you'll be all right if you've got what it takes? And do I have it, whatever it is? Do I, Evangeline Mudd, have what it takes?*

There was, of course, no way of knowing. She would to have to wait until she actually got to Ikkinasti to find out.

Chapter 13

It Seemed Very Odd to Her

When Dr. Pikkaflee said that the plane was waiting, Evangeline naturally assumed that she meant one of those big planes that hold hundreds of people and that serve you snacks like fizzy water and peanuts. But that wasn't what Aphrodite Pikkaflee meant. No, what she meant was a tiny little black thing covered with dents and scratches and chips parked at the end of a grassy runway in a field where cows and sheep were grazing. The plane, whose one wing was rust-colored and whose other wing was bright blue, reminded Evangeline so much of the little black car in which she had originally seen Dr. Pikkaflee that Evangeline wasn't at all sure that it *wasn't* the car with a couple of wings welded onto it. On both sides, just under the cockpit, THE FLYING MONKEY was painted in bright red letters.

"Well, what are you waiting for, dear?" Dr. Pikkaflee asked. "Hop in."

Within a matter of seconds, Evangeline was buckled up next to Dr. Pikkaflee, who was already in the pilot's seat fidgeting with all kinds of levers and buttons and dials.

Pansy had come along, too.

"We may need someone to copilot the plane in case of emergency," said Dr. Pikkaflee by way of explanation. "I once had a chimpanzee who was quite a natural pilot."

Evangeline had already developed a deep affection for Pansy and was delighted that she was going to accompany them to Ikkinasti, but in her heart of hearts she really did hope that it would not come to Pansy's copiloting *The Flying Monkey*.

It isn't that I don't trust her, Evangeline said to herself. *It's just that ... well ... she's an ape.*

"Unfortunately," Dr. Pikkaflee continued, "the chimp could never control his urge to loop-de-loop, so I had to ground him. Do you like to loop-de-loop, my dear?"

"I don't know," the girl honestly replied. "I've never done it."

"Well, we'll have to fix that, won't we?" said Dr. Pikkaflee.

And with that, *The Flying Monkey* left the ground, loop-de-looped once over the field, and headed straight in the direction of Ikkinasti.

Soon, the plane was darting and bobbing thousands of feet over the surface of the sea. Evangeline was enjoying herself immensely. Dr. Aphrodite Pikkaflee was an excellent traveling companion, and she didn't hesitate to talk about her many adventures searching for cotton-top tamarins on the banks of the Great Ooeygooey River or tracking highland gorillas through the wilds of the Bugabooboo Mountains.

Eventually, Evangeline lost count of the hours. Pansy settled down in her lap, and soon both girl and ape were fast asleep.

When Evangeline woke up, tiny brown dots of land were beginning to appear on the ocean below her. It looked as if someone had spilled a bag of chocolates on the surface of the water.

"Those are the Iddiebiddies," Dr. Pikkaflee explained. "We shall arrive in Bababun very soon."

Pansy seemed to understand what Dr. Pikkaflee had said. She sat up and looked ahead of her with one hand held up to her eyes to shield them from the glare.

She is looking for her parents, thought Evangeline. *She is looking for her parents just like I am looking for mine.*

"Evangeline, my dear," said Dr. Pikkaflee, as she pulled a knob that adjusted the flaps on *The Flying Monkey*'s wings, "would you mind showing me that postcard now? The one you received from your parents before they disappeared. I'd like to have a look at it."

Evangeline reached behind her and retrieved the postcard from its pocket in her pack. She handed the postcard to Dr. Pikkaflee.

"Is that your mother's drawing?" Dr. Pikkaflee asked, examining the postcard with both hands. This meant that for the moment nobody was actually piloting the plane. "Under the stamp, I mean."

"Yes," said Evangeline, noting that *The Flying Monkey* seemed to be descending rapidly. "She was always drawing golden-hairs. She did it all the time."

"Do you mind if I remove the stamp, my dear?" Dr. Pikkaflee asked. "I'd like to get a closer look."

Taking extra care not to destroy the drawing underneath it, Dr. Pikkaflee began to pick at the stamp. By now, *The Flying Monkey* was practically in a nosedive, a fact which Dr. Pikkaflee paid no attention whatever to, but which Evangeline couldn't help but take notice of. In spite of her nervousness, however, she was amazed at how Dr. Pikkaflee's enormous hands could do such delicate work. In a matter of seconds, Dr. Pikkaflee had peeled the stamp back far enough so that the golden-hair face beneath it was completely revealed.

"I knew that picking all those grubs out of tree bark would come in handy one day," she said. But then as she studied the drawing, her face began to grow more serious. "Evangeline, my dear," she said, handing the postcard back to the girl, "take a look at that drawing. Tell me what you see."

Evangeline took the postcard and studied the drawing. She recognized the dark, bold line with which Magdalena drew, and for a moment a heaviness filled her heart as she thought about those happy evenings in the cozy bungalow. Her mother had drawn the golden-hair with its brow wrinkled and its eyes squinting and looking off to the left. The longer the girl looked at the drawing, the more it seemed to be telling her something.

By now, *The Flying Monkey* was zooming straight toward the surface of the water. Dr. Pikkaflee, who had been studying Evangeline as Evangeline studied the postcard, grabbed hold of *The Flying Monkey*'s controls at last, and as the little plane first leveled itself and then began to climb, the message of the drawing became clear to Evangeline just as surely as if her mother had written it with words. It was as plain as the nose on Pansy's face.

"That's the face golden-hairs make when they are in danger!" she cried. "Magdalena was sending me a message. She was telling me that they were in trouble!"

"Yes," said Dr. Pikkaflee. "I'm afraid that she was."

"But I couldn't see it!" Evangeline continued. "She put the stamp over it."

"No, my dear," said Dr. Pikkaflee taking from the

pocket of her dress a postcard of her own. "That is where you are wrong. Your mother didn't put the stamp over the picture. Someone else did. Someone who didn't want you to see the picture at all."

She handed Evangeline a second postcard.

"I also received a postcard from your parents, my dear," she said. "It was mailed *two days* before yours was. Of course, I was able to read it only a few days ago."

Evangeline looked at the postcard. It appeared to be the same one her parents had sent her, but the message on the back was different.

We've already made a new friend here, it said, in Merriweather's straight up and down hand. *He's promised to guide us into the jungle to the very spot where the golden-hairs were reported to have been seen. His name is Rexi. P.S. He reminds us so much of you, Aphrodite. Isn't that odd?*

"But I don't understand," said Evangeline. "This postcard sounds like everything is fine."

"Yes," said Dr. Pikkaflee, "I suppose it would seem like that to anybody who didn't know Rexi."

"Rexi?" asked Evangeline. "You mean their new friend? The one who is going to guide them into the jungle?"

"Yes," said Dr. Pikkaflee. "Evangeline, it isn't so odd that he reminded your parents of me."

An unmistakable tone of sadness had crept into her voice.

"It isn't?" said Evangeline.

It seemed very odd to *her*. As far as *she* was concerned, there was no one on earth like Dr. Aphrodite Pikkaflee. No one.

"You see, Evangeline, dear," said Dr. Pikkaflee gravely. "Rexi is my brother."

Chapter 14

Pikkaflee's Paradise

It would be hard to describe all that went through Evangeline's head when she heard that Dr. Aphrodite Pikkaflee had a brother. The closest thing it can be compared to is the moment you discover that your teacher has a *first* name. Up to that time she had only been Miss Wangdoodle or Miss Buttonhole, and her sole purpose in life was to teach you to spell or to show you how to do subtraction. But once you actually hear someone, another teacher perhaps or maybe even your parents, call her "Desdemona" or "Winifred," all that changes. You suddenly realize that your teacher is *a person,* a person with a first name, a person who has a whole other life that has nothing to do with *you*. After that, the way you feel about your teacher can never be the same.

This is something like what Evangeline was feeling. Up to the very second Dr. Pikkaflee said that she had a brother, Evangeline had thought of her only as the person who had rescued her from Mudd's Manor, the person whose sole and utter purpose in life was to help her find out what happened to her parents. Now, as it turned out, Dr. Pikkaflee had a family of her own, a family that had nothing whatever to do with her, Evangeline Mudd.

One question after another began to jump into Evangeline's head. They were like people pouring from a crowded train onto the platform. *You have a brother? Is he an older brother or younger brother? How often do you see him? What does he look like? What about your parents?* These and hundreds more rushed out, but the first one that found its way from the platform to her mouth was:

"What is your brother doing in Ikkinasti?"

The Flying Monkey shuddered a bit as Dr. Pikkaflee caused it to drop altitude. Through the holes in the clouds, which seemed to be growing thicker and darker, Evangeline could see that the Iddiebiddies were gradually giving way to larger and larger islands.

"But Evangeline, dear," said Dr. Pikkaflee, "I thought you knew."

"Knew what?" Evangeline almost shouted. "I don't know anything!"

"Ikkinasti is my home," Dr. Pikkaflee replied. "It's where I grew up."

So that was the source of Dr. Pikkaflee's accent. Ikkinasti!

"Of course, I haven't lived there in years," Dr. Pikkaflee continued.

"Tell me," the girl demanded, hugging Pansy to her. "Tell me everything."

Dr. Pikkaflee fiddled with the controls and *The Flying Monkey* gradually began a descent through the clouds.

"There really isn't a great deal to tell," she began. "I was born in Bababun. My father was a fisherman. My mother kept a garden."

"What about Rexi?" Evangeline asked.

"Rexi came along when I was seven years old. He was a cunning baby. Everybody said so, and we thought he would grow up to do great things. Our first hint that perhaps we were wrong was when he spoke his first word."

"Mama?" Evangeline guessed.

Dr. Pikkaflee shook her head.

"Dada?"

"I'm afraid not," Dr. Pikkaflee said.

Evangeline tried one more time.

"Kitty?"

"No," said Dr. Pikkaflee. "Not *Mama* or *Dada* or *kitty*. *Money*. Rexi's first word was *money*."

Evangeline thought what with the roaring of the engines, she hadn't heard Dr. Pikkaflee properly.

"At first we tried to tell ourselves that he *was* trying to say *Mama*," Dr. Pikkaflee explained. "But it soon became clear that Mama wasn't enough for him. Nothing was. If my mother used the extra money she had earned at market to buy him a mango, he wanted two mangoes. If she bought him two mangoes, he wanted four. He was simply impossible to satisfy."

By now, *The Flying Monkey* was completely surrounded by the clouds. Outside the cockpit windows, the very air had turned white.

"Please don't stop," Evangeline said. "I want to know everything."

"Things went on this way for many years," Dr. Pikkaflee continued. "All of us trying to satisfy Rexi. Rexi never satisfied. Finally, after the Great Storm that destroyed our little bamboo house and carried my parents out to sea, I left Ikkinasti to become a primatologist."

"But what about Rexi?" Evangeline asked.

"He stayed on," said Dr. Pikkaflee. "He said that he had some plans that would finally put Ikkinasti on the map."

"What kind of plans?" Evangeline asked.

"Very bad plans, I'm afraid, Evangeline dear. You see, Rexi loved the jungle, too, but for a very different reason. He said that when he looked at the jungle, with each tree growing so close to the next, it always reminded him of something."

"What?" Evangeline asked. "What did it remind him of?"

"A wallet stuffed with money," Dr. Pikkaflee replied softly.

Dr. Pikkaflee cleared her throat, and Evangeline wasn't sure but thought she could see a tear forming in the corner of Dr. Aphrodite Pikkaflee's eye. After a moment in which Dr. Pikkaflee busied herself fidgeting with *The Flying Monkey*'s controls, she continued.

"One of his plans was to turn the jungle into an amusement park—Pikkaflee's Paradise, he called it.

He wanted to tear down all the trees and build the world's longest and highest roller coaster. Of course, he didn't get away with it. When I heard about it, I organized a resistance group, but in the end Rexi abandoned the idea of Pikkaflee's Paradise on his own."

Dr. Pikkaflee went back to fidgeting with the controls.

Evangeline remained silent. She knew that Dr. Pikkaflee would continue with her story when she was ready and able to. In the meantime, Evangeline concentrated on trying not to like the idea of the world's longest and highest roller coaster.

"Rexi realized that tourists are not apt to come to a place that is absolutely crawling with spiders who would like nothing better than to have them for lunch. It rather ruins a holiday."

For the first time since she had heard of them, Evangeline was grateful for the spiders. She didn't want to see one, of course, but she was glad they had thwarted Rexi's awful plan.

The ride was suddenly very bumpy. Pansy was clinging to her for dear life.

"Wh-at's Re-xi up to n-now?" Evangeline asked.

"I d-d-don't kno-o-w," Dr. Pikkaflee replied, "but whatever it is, it can't be any g-g-good." She grabbed a lever and slowly pushed it forward. *The Flying Monkey* trembled as it began a slow descent. "Hold on, dear—this part's a little tricky."

Evangeline grabbed hold of the seat bottom.

"Do you think . . . ?" she said. "Do you think he had anything to do with . . . with my parents' disappearing?"

"I can't say for certain," said Dr. Pikkaflee as she slowly pulled back the lever that lowered *The Flying Monkey*'s landing gear. "It's always a mistake to judge too quickly, but I have to admit that's what I'm afraid of."

Suddenly *The Flying Monkey* broke through its blanket of clouds. In spite of the heavy rain that pounded the plane from all sides, Evangeline could see a long, uneven shoreline. The sea that met it was dark and murky and lapped up onto the trunks of trees whose long, thin roots reached down into the water like the gnarled fingers of ancient monsters.

"Ikkinasti?" said Evangeline.

"Ikkinasti!" Dr. Pikkaflee responded.

Chapter 15

Bababun! Bababun! Bababun!

Now, if *you* were to hitch a ride on a bus with a young ape clinging to your neck, you might expect that your fellow passengers would sit up and take note. Could you blame them? Wouldn't *you* stare if the person who chose the seat next to yours was carrying an ape in her arms as though it was a googling baby? Of course you would. But that was not the case when Evangeline, Pansy, and Dr. Aphrodite Pikkaflee crammed their way onto the bus that was to take them from the dirt runway where *The Flying Monkey* had landed to the center of Bababun. No one paid the slightest bit of attention to them. In fact, it was Evangeline who was doing all the staring.

First off, to Evangeline the bus didn't appear to be a bus at all but instead some fantastic mix-up of jeep, fire engine, and carnival bumper car. Its sides and back were open, and it was painted with such bright pink-and-orange stripes that she had to squint every time she looked at it.

"Has a circus come to Ikkinasti?" Evangeline asked Dr. Aphrodite Pikkaflee, who had paid no attention whatever to the marvelous vehicle.

"A circus?" Dr. Pikkaflee answered. "Oh! You mean the jib-jib. It's our ride into town."

Then there was the birdcage mounted on the jib-jib's hood. In this cage sat an actual bird, a bird that Evangeline couldn't recognize. It was a big bird, huge in fact, almost the size of a turkey, with a violent red beak. Its feathers ranged in color from that of a ripe lime to a shimmering purple.

"I know it's not a sparrow or a robin or a chickadee," she said. "Perhaps it's a dodo."

"Bababun!" the bird squawked over and over. "Bababun! Bababun! Bababun!"

But if the outside of the bus was amazing to Evangeline, what it held inside was even more so. For the passengers had loaded it down with the most

astonishing array of
pigs
and chickens
and goats
and rice
and corn
and coconuts
and mangoes
and monkeys
and pineapples
and palms
and crates
and cartons
and baskets
and boxes

positively overflowing with all kinds of things. Things with leaves the size of tabletops and roots the size of footballs. Things that hooted and squawked. Things that chirped and crowed and yelped and barked. Things that Evangeline had no names for.

The passengers themselves scuttled in, around, and over this cargo, all the while shouting and laughing and arguing with one another over who was going to fit where. The roof of the jib-jib was just as crowded with passengers and their exotic belongings as the inside was. Passengers of all ages were hanging out the windows and clinging onto the back and sides. One man, barefoot and wearing a pair of ragged shorts and a T-shirt that said MY SON IS AN HONOR STUDENT AT BABABUN ELEMENTARY SCHOOL, had even climbed up onto the hood and was straddling the birdcage. It was as if there were a contest as to just how many passengers the vehicle could handle before it went crashing down over its tires onto the dusty ground.

There had been such a rush to get inside that Evangeline and Dr. Pikkaflee had become separated, and the girl found herself jammed between an ancient grandmother and a young goat. The grandmother was smoking a pipe and had holes in the tops of her ears through which she was carrying rolled-up wads of what Evangeline guessed was Ikkinasti money. In her arms she was cradling a pink-and-black pig that stared at Evangeline as if it would like nothing better than to take a chunk out of her nose. The goat was no better and actually did nibble Evangeline's dress once or twice.

Evangeline found all this remarkable until she remembered that she herself was holding an ape in her lap.

Why, I fit right in, she thought.

And she would have, too, if it hadn't been for the heat. No one else seemed to think anything of the

temperature on the bus, but to Evangeline it felt as if she were being roasted alive. Perspiration was popping out of every pore of her skin. She was soaked with it, especially since Pansy, unused to so much human activity, was hugging her even tighter. The pig especially seemed to find this objectionable and was looking at her more evilly than ever when the bus suddenly lurched forward and began its rollicking journey to Bababun.

Did my parents ride this same bus? thought Evangeline. *Did they hear the bird say, "Bababun! Bababun! Bababun!"? Did they sit next to pigs and goats? Did they see the lady with money in her ears?* And as these questions formed themselves, a new thought began to well up, not in her brain, where most thoughts come from, but in her heart. *Maybe,* she said to herself, *maybe I'll be able to ask them myself.*

This was almost the first time that Evangeline had allowed herself any hope that she might actually see her parents again, or at least the first time she had allowed herself to put that hope into words. But just for a moment, sitting between a pig and a goat, she did hope, she hoped with all her might. This, by the way, was no small thing.

Suddenly, the bus came to a screeching halt. A passenger carrying an entire bunch of bananas, a crate of coconuts, two geese, a monkey, and a pair of fat, laughing babies got off. The bird squawked. And, remarkably, three more passengers, who had been waiting patiently by the side of the road, got on.

The entire journey to Bababun was like this. Go forward ten feet. Stop. One person get off. Three people get on, each carrying a pig or a chicken or two chickens or in some cases what looked to be an entire flock of chickens. By the time the bus had reached its destination, Evangeline had disappeared into a blur of leaves and feathers and fur and trotters.

"Well, my dear," said Dr. Aphrodite Pikkaflee once they had finally alighted in the center of Bababun. "How did you like the ride?"

Evangeline pulled at her dress, which was now frayed at the edges.

She wanted to say that she thought if the passengers were going to bring goats onto the bus they should train them not to eat other passengers' clothing, but instead she took a more practical route.

"Hadn't we better get to our hotel?" she asked.

Dr. Pikkaflee looked around her as if for a moment she needed to take it all in.

"Yes, of course," she said. "You're right, my dear, absolutely right. "This is the first time I've been back here in a long time. But we've no time for reminiscing. First we'll get to our room and freshen up a bit and then . . ."

Here Dr. Pikkaflee hesitated.

"And then?" Evangeline asked.

"And then," Dr. Aphrodite Pikkaflee continued, "we had better find Rexi."

As the two gathered their bags and began to walk down Bababun's one street, Evangeline kept her eyes straight ahead. Earlier Dr. Pikkaflee had told her that the spitting spiders rarely ventured out of the jungle.

Just the same, the girl told herself, *it's best not to take any chances.*

Pansy, who was clinging to Evangeline's back, seemed to agree. She kept her eyes shut tight and opened them only when they got to the safety of the hotel.

Chapter 16

At the Ikkinasti House of Jungle Comfort

The room that Dr. Pikkaflee had referred to was in Bababun's only hotel, the Ikkinasti House of Jungle Comfort, which was neither a house nor a hotel, but like every other building in Bababun, as far as Evangeline could tell, a bamboo structure set up on stilts. Still, the room, with its bamboo walls and thatched ceiling, was the coolest place that Evangeline had been since she had arrived in Ikkinasti, and for this the girl was thankful. Even the lizards that ran up and down the walls didn't bother her much, once Dr. Pikkaflee had explained.

"They're just house lizards, Evangeline, dear," she had said, sitting down on one of the two bamboo platforms that Evangeline realized were the Jungle Comfort's idea of beds. "Nothing to worry about. You can look into their eyes as much as you want. They don't spit at all."

Evangeline was unacquainted with the term *house lizard*, and she hadn't really thought about looking into one's eyes, but it was a relief to know that should the occasion arise, it would be safe to do so.

Pansy had swung up and settled onto one of the large bamboo crossbeams that ran from the top of one thatched wall to another. Evangeline had been surprised that no one at the hotel had objected to Pansy. Apparently, apes were regular guests at the Ikkinasti House of Jungle Comfort.

Once Dr. Pikkaflee had awakened the boy who was sleeping at the bamboo desk by announcing her name, there was an even bigger surprise. The boy, who looked to Evangline to be younger than herself, reached under the desk and handed Dr. Pikkaflee a plain white envelope.

"For me?" she had said. "Surely there must be some mistake."

But there was no mistake. Her name was scrawled across the envelope in thick, black letters. Dr. Pikkaflee did not open the envelope immediately. It was only after they had gotten comfortably settled into their room that she picked it up from the bamboo stand where she had laid it.

"Now," she said, "let's see what this is all about. I have a feeling that I know who it's from."

She opened the envelope and pulled out a sheet of white paper folded neatly in three. This she handed to Evangeline.

"Would you read it to me, dear?" she asked. "My eyes are rather tired after all that flying."

Evangeline took the sheet of paper and unfolded it. The first thing she did was look at the signature.

"It's from Rexi!" she told Dr. Pikkaflee.

"I thought so," responded the doctor.

"But how did he even know we were here?" asked Evangeline. "Did you tell him we were coming?"

"Of course not," Dr. Aphrodite Pikkaflee said. "I didn't have to. He has always had spies all over

Bababun. When *The Flying Monkey* landed, he was probably the first to know it. It was someone on the bus, no doubt."

Is it possible? Evangeline wondered. *Can an old lady who smokes a pipe and carries a pig also be a spy?*

Life, she decided, was very mysterious.

"He would naturally leave the letter at the Ikkinasti House of Jungle Comfort, because it's the only hotel in town. He knew this is where we would be. Let's hear what the rascal has to say."

Evangeline cleared her throat, but before she read the first word, she stopped. Her face, already pink from the sun, turned even pinker.

"What is it, child?" Dr. Pikkaflee asked.

"It's just that . . . well, I'm afraid the letter doesn't begin very nicely," she said.

"I should have guessed," Dr. Pikkaflee responded. "Don't worry, Evangeline, dear. I'm used to it. Don't forget, Rexi is my brother."

"Are you sure?" Evangeline asked. "Are you sure you won't get mad?"

"Quite sure," Dr. Pikkaflee answered. "Now go ahead."

Evangeline cleared her throat a second time and began.

"Dear Aphro . . . Aphroditzy!" she read.

"If you've come to find the new family of golden-hairs, forget it! I made the whole thing up when I was planning to turn the jungle into the WORLD'S BIGGEST MALL. I knew that you'd try to stop me, just like you tried to stop me when I wanted to build Pikkaflee's Paradise. *I also knew if you heard about a new family of your beloved apes, you'd come back to Ikkinasti to try and find them. Once you got here, I was going to . . . well, I wasn't sure what I was going to do, but I don't think you would have liked it.*

When that drippy Mudd couple turned up instead, I pretended to be their friend until I could decide what to do. Finally, I realized that if they went missing, you'd show up sooner or later, so I took them out to a part of the jungle from which I knew they could never find their way back and left them there. Pity, isn't it? I'm sure the spiders didn't think so. By the way, as you can see, the plan for the WORLD'S BIGGEST MALL didn't work out, but don't worry, my new scheme is even better.

So, sister dear, the best thing for you to do is get back in that rattletrap you call an airplane

and get out of here. Oh, and on your way, you
can kiss that jungle out there goodbye.
Rexi
P.S. Who is that nasty-looking little runt
you're dragging around with you?"

Evangeline, who had been standing as she read, sat down on the bamboo platform next to Dr. Pikkaflee's. What was it that Rexi had written about her parents . . . ? *I took them out to a part of the jungle from which I knew they could never find their way back and left them there.* He was right, of course. No one could survive in that jungle.

"Now, now," said Dr. Pikkaflee, getting up and putting her arms around the girl. "You mustn't take what Rexi has said to heart. Your parents are very clever people, Evangeline."

"But it's been such a long time," said Evangeline, "such a very long time and there are so many spiders. Even you said so."

"That's true," Dr. Pikkaflee replied. "But which do you believe in most? The spiders? Or your parents?"

Put that way, Evangeline had no choice.

"Now, come along, child," Dr. Pikkaflee exclaimed, jumping up from the bed. "We have to find Dadoo."

"Who?" asked Evangeline.

"An old friend of mine," Dr. Pikkaflee answered, as she headed toward the door. "He'll take us into the jungle. He was raised there. If your parents are in there, Evangeline, dear, Dadoo will find them."

Evangeline pulled herself together and stood up.

"By the way," Dr. Pikkaflee added cheerfully, "you don't have anything against headhunters, do you?"

Chapter 17

Naughties!

E vangeline decided that she didn't have anything against headhunters, especially if one were going to help her find her parents. Still, she had never met a headhunter before. There had been no opportunity for meeting one at Mudd's Manor, and, as far as she knew, her parents had had no friends who were headhunters. (Do yours?) This, she felt, was a great pity, because if they had, then she would know how to behave when she was introduced to Dadoo.

"Dr. Pikkaflee," said the girl as the two slowly walked down Bababun's one street. Pansy had stayed behind at the Ikkinasti House of Jungle Comfort. "Does Dadoo still . . . er . . . you know."

"Take heads, you mean?" her friend replied. "He gave up headhunting years ago, I think."

It was not entirely clear to Evangeline whether that *I think* meant:

1. *I think* it was years ago that he gave up headhunting;

or

2. *I think* he gave up headhunting.

These two are of course very, very different, and if you had been Evangeline, you might have pressed Dr. Pikkaflee further in an effort to find out which one she meant. But Evangeline decided not to think about it. She did hope, though, that Dadoo would find *her* head of no particular interest.

Eventually, the two came to the end of the street, where they were met by a wall of green. It was the jungle growing right up to the edge of Bababun. Trees, far taller than those that grew around Mudd's Manor or the cozy bungalow in New England, reached up into the sky, and from the dark canopy above hung creepers and vines. Orchids were growing out of the trunks of some of the trees, and on others great fanlike structures sprouted.

"Dadoo's longhouse used to be right through here," said Dr. Pikkaflee as she stepped into the dark shade. "I hope he hasn't moved."

Evangeline was about to follow her friend when she was prevented from doing so by a figure that seemed to appear out of nowhere. The man, for it was a man, stood directly in the middle of the path as if he had been there for all time, though Evangeline was absolutely certain that a second before there had been no one there except Dr. Pikkaflee. He was wearing nothing more than shorts and a pair of ancient tennis shoes with no laces and so many holes that various toes stuck out as if they were making a break from the shreds of canvas and rubber that surrounded them.

For a moment, he stood there staring at Evangeline, who could do nothing but stare back. Still, she had the idea that he was waiting for something.

"Naughties," he said at last. "You very naughties."

Startled as she was, Evangeline was about to reply to this peculiar creature that she thought it was *he* who was naughty, frightening little girls by appearing right before their eyes like that. But, on second thought, she decided it was perhaps not the best idea to get into an argument with a stranger when there were headhunters about. (This is good advice, by the way. Follow it whenever you can.)

"Dr. Pikkaflee!" she called out. "Help!"

Later, Evangeline was very angry with herself for calling out like that. After all, the man hadn't done anything except stand there.

Was it the tattoos, the ears, or the blowpipe that caused me to do it? she wondered later. And she promised herself not to call out for help automatically the next time she met someone who was covered from head to foot in tattoos and whose earlobes were looped over the tops of his ears and who was carrying a very long and dangerous-looking blowpipe over his shoulder.

"Ah, Evangeline," said Dr. Pikkaflee as she came scurrying back. "What a clever girl you are! You've found Dadoo!"

Dadoo stared straight into Evangeline's eyes.

"She very naughties," he said.

"Nonsense, Dadoo," said Dr. Pikkaflee cheerfully. "You're too sensitive. After all, the girl hasn't had many opportunities to see such a handsome fellow as you."

Dr. Pikkaflee took a step backward and with an elegant flourish of her enormous hand made a proper introduction.

"Evangeline Mudd, permit me to introduce Dadoo," she said. "Dadoo . . . Evangeline Mudd."

"It's very nice to meet you, Mr. Dadoo," Evangeline said, hoping with all her might that this was the way a headhunter liked to be greeted.

Unfortunately for the girl, it didn't seem to be.

Dadoo furrowed his brow and grimaced in a way that managed to show all his teeth at once, teeth that, Evangeline couldn't help but notice, had been filed into sharp points.

"Naughties," Dadoo repeated. "Very naughties."

"In Dadoo's society, Evangeline, dear," Dr. Pikkaflee gently explained, "it's customary for children to show respect to their elders by touching foreheads. It's considered very rude if you don't."

From the moment Evangeline had learned that she was going to Ikkinasti, she had prepared herself. She had prepared herself for the little wormy things and for the huge mosquitoes and even for the spiders. But there was nothing, nothing at all, that she could have done to prepare herself for touching foreheads with a headhunter.

"Couldn't we just shake hands instead?" Evangeline asked.

"Oh, good heavens no!" Dr. Pikkaflee replied. "Whatever you do, don't extend your hand! In Dadoo's society that's an invitation to a wrestling match!"

In the end, Evangeline decided that touching foreheads with a headhunter was much better than wrestling with one, and so taking a small step forward and standing on her toes, she closed her eyes and touched Dadoo's forehead with her own.

This appeared to do the trick. Dadoo was beaming.

"Betters," he said. "Now you goods girl."

Evangeline was very happy to hear Dadoo's new assessment of her character, though she thought to herself that if all it took to make naughty children good was to touch a headhunter's forehead, it might be good to have headhunters on every street corner.

The three walked to Dadoo's longhouse, which, as Dr. Pikkaflee had said, was just through the jungle wall. The longhouse itself was not so different from the Ikkinasti House of Jungle Comfort, except that it had no furniture and it seemed much, much older. From the crossbeams hung bundles wrapped in coconut and banana fronds. Evangeline couldn't help but wonder what those bundles contained. They were just about the size of . . . well, they were head-sized.

Dr. Pikkaflee and Dadoo spoke in a language that Evangeline couldn't understand and, as far as she knew, had never heard. It contained all kinds of clicking and humming and buzzing noises.

Eventually, the two stopped talking, and Dr. Pikkaflee turned to Evangeline.

"We leave tomorrow morning," she said. "Dadoo has agreed to take us deep into the jungle to see if we can discover what may have happened to your parents. It's a very dangerous journey, Evangeline. Are you sure you're up to it?"

Evangeline looked at Dr. Pikkaflee and Dadoo.

"I've come this far," she said. "I'm not turning back now."

"You goods girl." Dadoo beamed. "Very, very goods."

Chapter 18

Toothpicks R Us

The next morning at five o'clock, Dr. Aphrodite Pikkaflee, Evangeline, and Pansy met Dadoo at his longhouse. This time Evangeline knew exactly what to do, and without the slightest hesitation she walked up to the headhunter and touched his forehead with her own. This pleased Dadoo immensely.

"Terrifics!" he shouted. "You terrifics, excellents, and very greats."

"You, too," Evangeline shouted back. She meant it. She did consider Dadoo to be terrific. After all, he had agreed to take them into the jungle to find her parents, and if his earlobes touched his shoulders and he carried a blowpipe—what of it?

With the greetings out of the way, Dadoo picked up a huge bundle, almost as big as Evangeline herself, and put it on his head.

"Foods," he announced.

The bundle balanced perfectly. It was as if it had been a hat especially fitted for him.

"Walks now," Dadoo said, and with that, the long, dangerous journey into the jungle began.

They walked in single file with Dadoo leading the way, followed by Evangeline, Dr. Pikkaflee, and finally Pansy, who dawdled along behind, looking under leaves, sniffing twigs, and generally goofing around in the way that young golden-hairs like to do.

At first, Evangeline held back. Not from fear of the jungle and all it contained, but from fear that the bundle balancing on Dadoo's head was going to fall on her. It soon became clear to her, however, that Dadoo's step was so sure that the huge load was going to stay exactly where it was.

"How does he do it?" Evangeline asked Dr. Pikkaflee. "How does he keep that bundle on his head?"

"Try it yourself, dear, and find out," Dr. Pikkaflee suggested. "All it takes is a little concentration, a little balance, and a little practice."

Evangeline immediately slipped off her backpack and put it on her head. At first, she could take no more

than three steps without it falling off, but by looking straight ahead and imitating the way Dadoo stepped along so naturally, she began to get the hang of it.

She wanted to shout to the others, "Hey! Look at me! Look what I can do!" She was about to do it, too, until she remembered India Terpsichore bouncing around the kitchen like an antelope and demanding that Evangeline watch every step she take.

They were traveling on a well-worn path, and so, although Dadoo kept them going at a fast clip, the walking itself was not so difficult, and by moving her head very slowly to the right or left, Evangeline had time to look around her as they moved along.

Everywhere her eyes fell, something was growing, something short or something tall, something spiky or something rounded, something scalloped or something arrow-shaped. It was mostly green, but there were drifts and splotches of color, too—reds and purples and pinks and oranges—where flowers the size of cabbages were blooming.

Just as amazing as the flowers, though, were the tattoos that covered Dadoo's back. Evangeline had seen one or two tattoos in her life but they were of the usual kind—an anchor or heart with a banner across it that said MOTHER.

Dadoo's tattoos were nothing like those. In fact,

Dadoo's tattoos were not pictures of things at all, but instead a series of swirling shapes that whirled and curlicued across his back and up and down his spine. It reminded Evangeline of pictures of outer space she had seen in books, with one galaxy spiraling after another, except that in those pictures all the galaxies looked the same. As she looked carefully at Dadoo's back, though, she realized that each tattoo was slightly different from the next, just in the way that snowflakes are.

"Dadoo?" Evangeline asked as they marched along. "What do those tattoos mean?"

Dadoo stopped so abruptly that the girl very nearly ran into him.

He turned around to face her.

"Every time Dadoo get trophies, Dadoo get tatooies," he said proudly. "Many lotsa trophies. Many lotsa tatooies."

"Trophies?" Evangeline asked. "You mean like bowling trophies or basketball trophies?"

Admittedly, this seemed highly unlikely to the girl. It was very improbable that there even was a bowling alley in Bababun, but Dadoo had said *trophies* and she couldn't think what else people got trophies for.

"Bowlings?" Dadoo asked. "Basketsballs?"

"Evangeline, dear . . . ," said Dr. Pikkaflee from

behind. "When Dadoo talks about getting trophies, he doesn't mean the usual kind of trophy. He means, well . . . he means . . ."

Dr. Pikkaflee didn't have to finish her sentence. Evangeline knew what she meant without further explanation. Those bundles hanging from the rafters in Dadoo's longhouse explained it all.

Evangeline gulped.

"You mean . . . you mean . . ." She couldn't quite bring herself to say it.

"I'm afraid so," said Dr. Pikkaflee.

"Dadoo no gets trophies no mores," he said sadly. "Dadoo very friendlies now."

"Er . . . that's very nice, Dadoo," said Evangeline. "I think it's very good to be friendly."

"Yes," said Dadoo. "Goods but borings."

And with that, he turned and resumed walking.

Evangeline decided that perhaps it was best not to ask Dadoo any more questions.

They walked for several hours, remaining on the path and saying very little, but that didn't mean they were walking in silence. What with the insects humming and buzzing and beeping and chirping, and the birds squawking and hooting and whistling and warbling, and the monkeys howling and squealing and screeching and screaming, Evangeline decided that the jungle was the noisiest place she had ever been.

But soon the girl became aware of another noise that could be heard under the natural racket of the jungle. At first, she thought it was thunder, but the noise was too long and too steady for that. The noise seemed especially frightening to Pansy, who ran from her place behind Dr. Pikkaflee and jumped, whimpering, into Evangeline's arms.

Dadoo stopped and listened. Now that they had stopped walking, Evangeline could concentrate on the noise itself.

"Bads!" said Dadoo. "Very terribles and bads."

"What is it, Dr. Pikkaflee?" Evangeline asked.

"I don't know, dear," Dr. Pikkaflee replied. "It almost sounds like motors running. Huge motors!"

Dadoo resumed walking, though not so quickly as before. Within a few minutes, they came to the edge of the clearing, and it was obvious to all what was making the noise. Bulldozers! Big yellow bulldozers. They were pushing over trees. Hundreds of them.

Evangeline watched in horror as one of these machines ran up to a tree whose canopy held a mother monkey and her baby. Pansy, who was still in Evangeline's arms, whimpered. Evangeline closed her eyes when the tree fell with a terrible crash. She didn't see what had happened to the baby monkey or its mother.

When she opened her eyes again, she saw that in the middle of the destruction was a small man wearing a beret and sunglasses. He was sitting in a chair with a canvas back and seat, like the kind that movie directors sit in. It seemed to Evangeline that he was telling the bulldozers what to do through the means of a walkie-talkie. Every time a tree fell to the ground, the little man jumped up and clicked his heels in the air.

It was while she was watching the insane antics of this terrible man that Evangeline noticed what was printed in bright red letters on the sides of the big yellow bulldozers. R. PIKKAFLEE & COMPANY, she read. TOOTHPICKS R US.

Chapter 19

Goo-Goo Juice!

"It's Rexi!" Evangeline shouted over the noise of the trucks and the falling trees.

"Yes," Dr. Pikkaflee shouted back. "I'm afraid that it is."

"That's what he meant in the letter when he said there won't be any jungle left," said Evangeline. "He's turning it into toothpicks! He's going to knock down all the trees and make toothpicks out of them!"

"Yes," said Dr. Pikkaflee sadly. "It seems that he is."

"We can't let him do that!" Evangeline shouted. "We've got to stop him!"

"I'm afraid we're too late, Evangeline," said Dr.

Pikkaflee. "There's nothing we can do about it. At least for the moment."

Up to this point, Dadoo had said nothing, but now he turned to Dr. Pikkaflee and put his bundle on the ground.

"You wrongs," he said. "You very most extremely wrongs. Dadoo do somethings. Dadoo do somethings right now."

In a matter of seconds, Dadoo walked over to one of the trees at the edge of the clearing and climbed it so quickly that he had already come back down by the time Evangeline and Dr. Aphrodite Pikkaflee realized what he had done. In his hand, he held a small green leaf that he had plucked from one of the vines climbing near the top of the tree. This he crushed between his thumb and forefinger.

"What's he doing?" Evangeline asked Dr. Pikkaflee.

"I'm not sure," Dr. Pikkaflee replied. "But I don't think I like it."

Dadoo continued to crush the leaf until it looked like he had a big blob of bright green toothpaste right in the middle of his palm.

Next, he took his blowpipe from his shoulder and smeared the paste onto the tip of one of the long, slender darts that he had removed from its quiver.

"Dadoo mads now," he said. "Very extremely mads."
Dr. Pikkaflee looked alarmed.

"Now, Dadoo, you mustn't," she said. "You have
given all that up, remember?"

"Yes," said Evangeline quickly. "Remember you
said that you were friendly now. No more . . . er . . .
trophies."

But before Evangeline or Dr. Aphrodite Pikkaflee
could do anything to stop him, Dadoo had lifted the
blowpipe to his lips, puffed out his cheeks, and with a
huge gust of air sent the dart flying. It flew through
the air straight and true until it found its mark in Rexi
Pikkaflee's bottom.

Rexi dropped the
walkie-talkie and
made a swat at his
backside as if he had
been stung by a bee.
"You've poisoned
Rexi!" shouted
Evangeline.
"You've
shot a
poison dart into
Rexi's bottom!"
"Not poison,"

Dadoo replied, holding up his thumb and finger, which were still stained with the green paste. "Goo-goo juice!"

"Goo-goo juice?" Evangeline asked. "What's that?"

"You watch now," said Dadoo.

Evangeline turned to see that Rexi was grinning from ear to ear, as if he were a kid whose costume had just won first prize in a Halloween parade. He was marching around in a tiny circle. Occasionally he gave a skip. It almost looked as if he were making up a ridiculous little dance.

Evangeline watched in fascination as the dance became more and more intricate. Rexi bobbed back and forth. He hopped on one leg and then on the other. He twirled around and around. And every so often he would skip in a circle and then at the most unexpected moment hop into its center as if there were other invisible dancers all about to do the same.

To Evangeline, it looked like Rexi was trying to do the bunny hop and the hokey-pokey at the same time.

"What's wrong with Rexi?" she asked Dadoo. "Why is he acting like that?"

"He goo-goos now," said Dadoo, smiling. "He dancing goo-goo dance."

Rexi picked up the walkie-talkie and began to shout into it. The drivers of the bulldozers, under strict instructions to follow Rexi's every order, began to move the bulldozers in time to Rexi's commands. They went back. They went forth. They went fast. They went slow. They went around and around. But going around and around in the bulldozers made the drivers so dizzy that when, still following Rexi's instructions, they met in the middle, it was in one gigantic bulldozer crash. The bulldozers piled up on top of one another, smoking and grinding in a huge yellow tangle.

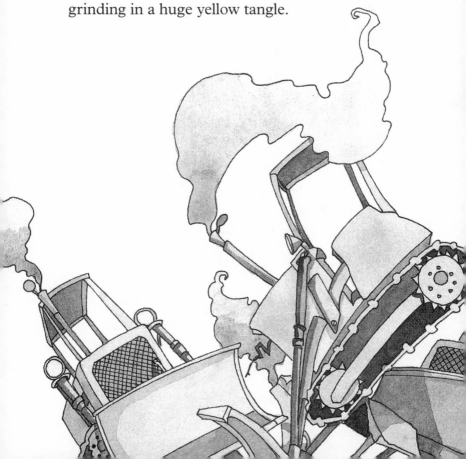

Rexi ran over to the gigantic jumble.

"You guys are a riot!" He giggled. "You're hilarious! You crack me up. Let's do it again!"

And once more, he started the goo-goo dance.

The drivers, unsure of what to do next, hopped out of the machines and formed a line behind him. Soon, they were all doing the goo-goo dance.

"He no more knocks trees today," said Dadoo, picking up the bundle and putting it back on his head.

"But how long will he be goo-goo?" asked Evangeline. "Will it be forever?"

"Not forevers," Dadoo replied. "Two maybes three hours. Then he be him uglies self again."

"And once he is himself, he'll realize what's happened. He won't be happy," said Dr. Pikkaflee, her brow furrowed with worry. "Make no mistake about it. We haven't seen the last of Rexi."

"We walks now," said Dadoo.

The others followed as Dadoo found his way through the clearing, which was as wide as a football field and much more difficult to maneuver than the jungle on either side. The travelers had to make their way over, around, and under the thousands of trees that Rexi and his men had knocked over.

When Evangeline was in the middle of the clearing, she stopped to catch her breath. But what she saw didn't provide her with any peace. On either side of her, Rexi and his bulldozers had knocked down the jungle as far as she could see. There were no living plants. No insects. No birds. No monkeys. No life at all. Just a ring of bare, red earth crisscrossed with the trunks of the fallen trees.

"Oh, Pansy," the girl cried to the little ape who had returned to her side. "What has Rexi done?"

"Keep moving, Evangeline, dear," said Dr. Pikkaflee. "We don't want to be spotted by the goo-goo dancers."

It was with a very heavy heart that Evangeline took Pansy's hand and forced herself to move on.

Chapter 20
They Are Human!

On the other side of the clearing, the jungle became much thicker. Soon, the path disappeared altogether. Pansy had stopped walking and was instead following along in the treetops, swinging and hopping from branch to branch. It would have been easier for Evangeline to brachiate, too, and she was just about to suggest it when she thought of the spiders. What would she do if she were hundreds of feet above the forest floor and she ran into one of the spitting spiders of Ikkinasti?

I'd better stay on the ground, she thought.

As she trudged along behind Dadoo, it occurred to the girl that she didn't have the slightest idea where they were going. They had come into the jungle to look for her parents, but what was their destination?

"Dr. Pikkaflee?" she asked. "Where is Dadoo taking us?"

"I really hadn't thought about it, child," Dr. Pikkaflee replied. "But Dadoo knows this jungle as if it were his own backyard. He was raised in it. If he says he can find your parents, then I'll bet *The Flying Monkey* that he can."

Dadoo himself then said something in his own language.

"By the way, dear," Dr. Pikkaflee added, "Dadoo says to keep your eyes on the path. We're in spider territory now."

Evangeline tried so hard not to look up that her neck began to ache. But above her, the canopy rustled with the animals and birds that were living there. To Evangeline, the jungle was beginning to seem like an animal itself. One huge animal, made up of thousands and thousands of different parts, leaves and feathers and fur and wings and flowers and roots all connected to each other in some mysterious way. It reminded her, too, of some of the music Madame Valentina Kloudishskaya would play for her during her lessons.

"You see, Evangeline," the great teacher would say, "each hand is making its own melody. Each finger is playing its own note, but to make beautiful music they must all come together to form something completely new."

Evangeline began to think of the jungle as a great symphony. She could feel its rhythms and its rests, its harmonies and its dissonance, its tempos and its dynamics. Every insect, no matter how small, every animal, no matter how ferocious, played its part in the symphony. The plants played their part, too, the sharp grasses and the soft mosses, the flowers, the thorns, and the trees, especially the trees.

Eventually, Dadoo led them to the bank of a river.

"We rests now," he said, putting down the bundle on a large rock.

Evangeline couldn't have imagined any words sweeter than those three. She was utterly exhausted. She plopped down onto one of the rocks. Within seconds she was asleep and dreaming.

She dreamed that she was back in Dr. Pikkaflee's tree house, swinging in the hammock. But in her dream the arc of the swing was much, much bigger. It felt as if she were swinging from one side of the room to the other.

"Wheeeeee!" she cried out. "Wheeeeee!"

Evangeline couldn't remember at exactly which point in the dream she woke up to discover that she *was* swinging. She was in the canopy of the jungle swinging from branch to branch and tree to tree. She was whisking through the jungle, in the arms of a full-grown golden-haired ape!

Now, I don't know how many of you have awakened from a lovely dream to discover that you have been snatched in your sleep by a four-hundred-pound ape whizzing you through the rain forest. If you have, you will know exactly how Evangeline felt when she discovered what was happening.

"Dadoo!" Evangeline cried out. "Dr. Pikkaflee!"

"Evangeline! Evangeline, dear, are you all right?"

It was Dr. Pikkaflee's voice. Evangeline was certain of that, but she couldn't tell where the voice was coming from. It sounded near, but that would have been impossible.

"I think so," Evangeline cried out. "I mean, I'm not hurt or anything, but I'm being carried through the jungle by a golden-hair!"

"I know, dear," said Dr. Pikkaflee. "I am very aware of your predicament. I'd offer some assistance, but I myself am rather indisposed at the moment."

Evangeline turned her head to see that Dr. Pikkaflee herself had been snatched and was in the arms of an ape very similar to Evangeline's.

"What's going on?" Evangeline asked.

154

"I wish I knew," said Dr. Pikkaflee.

"What about Dadoo?" Evangeline called out. "Do they have him, too?"

"I don't think so," Dr. Pikkaflee shouted. "But I can't be sure."

"And what about Pansy?"

But this question was answered by Pansy herself, who came swinging along, working hard to keep up with the two that had snatched Evangeline and Dr. Pikkaflee.

"Dr. Pikkaflee?" Evangeline called out once more. "What should we do?"

"I'm not sure there is anything we *can* do," Dr. Pikkaflee answered. "Perhaps the best thing is to just sit back and enjoy the ride."

This seemed very sensible advice to the girl. Certainly, it didn't make sense to struggle, since if the golden-hair should drop her, the fall to the jungle floor would have been . . . She decided she wouldn't think about that.

The ape itself had a very firm hold of Evangeline but was not squeezing her so tightly that it was uncomfortable. Still, apes are not known to bathe as frequently as you or I might, so the smell of a four-hundred-pound ape was not nearly as nice as Evangeline wished it had been.

They traveled like this for what seemed like hours. Leaves and vines and flowers whizzed by. Up and down, and forward, always forward. Occasionally, Evangeline would come face to face with a marmoset or a tamarin who looked extremely irritated to have its privacy so rudely interrupted by a ten-year-old girl who, after all, had no business sticking her nose into its business.

Several times, Evangeline tried to apologize, but by the time the words came out she was already in the next tree.

Eventually, the apes began to slow, and before she could realize what was happening, Evangeline was standing next to Dr. Pikkaflee in a large clearing. The trees that surrounded it were so tall that it seemed their crowns were very nearly in the clouds.

The golden-hairs, having run into the forest, were nowhere to be seen.

"That was lovely!" Dr. Pikkaflee exclaimed. "Absolutely first-rate! And, oh, what I've learned about the ways golden-hairs travel. You won't see me falling out of any trees for a long time to come, I can tell you."

Evangeline's legs were a little wobbly, the way legs tend to be after spending a long time on a ship. But after a step or two on solid ground, the girl was as steady as ever. She looked around to see that she and Dr. Pikkaflee were standing near a lovely, clear pool fed by a stream bubbling up out of the jungle.

Evangeline thought her eyes were playing tricks on her because at the other end of the stream she thought she saw what looked like a hut.

But it can't be, she told herself, *not here.*

She was about to point out the mirage to Dr. Pikkaflee when two golden-hairs walked out of the hut. At least she thought they were golden-hairs. One thing was certain. They weren't the apes that had carried them there. These apes were much smaller, and though they were far away, it seemed to Evangeline that they weren't nearly as hairy, either.

They almost look human, thought Evangeline. *In fact . . . in fact . . . they are human!*

"Merriweather!" she cried out. "Magdalena!"

For it was true. The golden-hairs had brought Evangeline to her beloved parents, Merriweather and Magdalena Mudd.

Chapter 21

I See What You Mean

It would be impossible to describe the reunion that Evangeline had with her parents. There was so much crying and laughing and hugging and nose rubbing that it went on far into the night. Dr. Aphrodite Pikkaflee wasn't excluded from these goings-on, either. Magdalena and Merriweather were delighted to see their mentor again, even if it was in a hut in the middle of the Ikkinasti Jungle.

Evangeline told her parents all about her life at Mudd's Manor, and they told her all about the months they had spent in the jungle.

"It's the golden-hairs," Merriweather said. "When

Rexi abandoned us, the golden-hairs found us and brought us here, just like they brought you."

"But how have you lived?" Dr. Aphrodite Pikkaflee asked. "How have you eaten?"

"The golden-hairs again!" Magdalena answered. "They bring us our food." This was astounding news!

"You mean the golden-hairs are taking care of you?" Dr. Pikkaflee was practically shouting.

"We've become quite good friends," Merriweather said. "There's a great deal about golden-haired apes that you don't know, Aphrodite. We've been to some jolly golden-hair parties in the last four months, let me tell you. You wouldn't believe how these apes can bugaloo. But whatever you do, don't play monkey tag with them. They cheat."

"You played monkey tag with the golden-hairs?" Evangeline asked.

"It helped to pass the time," said Magdalena.

"Of course, we didn't call it monkey tag," Merriweather continued. "As it turns out, golden-hairs are extremely sensitive."

"Still," Magdalena went on. "They're quite the party animals, if you'll pardon the expression. We plan to write a book about it if we ever get home."

Evangeline couldn't believe what she was hearing. This was too much.

"You mean all the time Melvin Mudd was bouncing ideas off me, you two were here playing games with golden-haired apes?" she said. "You mean you left me to play piano for India Terpsichore for hours on end so that you could have fun with the apes?"

Dr. Pikkaflee looked at the floor of the hut and pretended that there was something very interesting down there that she needed to concentrate on.

"But, Evangeline, darling," Magdalena said, "we were just trying to make the best of a bad situation. Don't you see?"

"No!" Evangeline shouted. "No! I don't see! I don't see at all!"

"Darling," Magdalena replied softly, "you don't understand."

"Understand what?" Evangeline shouted again. "There's nothing to understand!"

"We thought about you every single day," said Magdalena, hugging Evangeline tightly to her.

"Every single day, every single hour, every single minute, every single second," Merriweather added, hugging her even tighter.

"Then why didn't you come and get me?" asked Evangeline. "Why did you leave me at Mudd's Manor?"

"We would have come, darling," her mother said. "We would have if we could have."

"But why couldn't you?"

Merriweather looked at Magdalena. Magdalena looked at Merriweather. Evangeline remembered that moment, months ago, when they told her that she couldn't accompany them to the Ikkinasti Jungle.

"Because, Evangeline," her father finally said, "the golden-hairs won't let us leave. We are their prisoners!"

For a moment, no one said anything. Even the jungle seemed to quiet down at this important news.

Evangeline herself was dumbstruck. Of course her parents would have come to get her if they could have. Of course they wouldn't have left her to suffer at Mudd's Manor.

But Dr. Aphrodite Pikkaflee, sympathetic as she was to the misunderstanding between Evangeline and her mother and father, was still recovering from the news itself.

"What do you mean the golden-hairs won't let you leave?" she asked.

"I mean every time we try to leave the clearing, they pick us up and bring us back," said Merriweather. "They're very gentle about it, but they're also quite firm."

"But why?" Dr. Pikkaflee asked. "Why are they keeping you here?"

"We don't know," Magdalena explained. "They seem to think it's some kind of game. A kind of golden-hair hide-and-seek."

"It's rather fun, actually," Merriweather added. "If it weren't so frustrating, that is."

He cast a guilty look at Evangeline.

But by now, Evangeline was thinking of other things.

"With Rexi planning to tear down the jungle for toothpicks, there won't be any more hide-and-seek," she said.

"Toothpicks?" Magdalena and Merriweather asked together. After all, they had been living in the jungle for four months. They had no idea what Rexi was up to.

Evangeline told her parents about Rexi's latest plan. She even told them about watching the bulldozer push the tree over with the monkey and her baby.

"It's a disaster!" said Merriweather.

"It's a calamity!" said Magdalena.

"It's ridiculous!" said Dr. Aphrodite Pikkaflee. "I refuse to be kept in a human zoo. No ape is going to keep me here, and to prove it, I'm going to march out of here right now. I'll get to Bababun, and when I do, I'll send for help for you all."

"It's quite useless, you know," said Merriweather. "We've tried to escape every day since the day we arrived."

"Sometimes twice a day," Magdalena agreed. "And each time we have been caught by the golden-hairs and deposited right here in this hut."

"Just let them try that with me," said Dr. Aphrodite Pikkaflee, and without another word she squared her shoulders and walked out the door.

"She's very determined," said Evangeline.

"Yes, she is," her parents agreed.

In approximately three minutes, there was a gentle thud outside the door.

Dr. Aphrodite Pikkaflee walked in.

"I see what you mean," she said.

Chapter 22

Goodbye, Pansy!

Very early the next morning Evangeline awakened to find her parents and Dr. Pikkaflee already up and moving about. They were eating a fruit salad that, just as Magdalena had explained, had been brought by the golden-hairs. It was a lovely salad with mangoes and bananas and pineapples and other fruits that Evangeline couldn't recognize.

"You really should try some of this, my dear," said Dr. Pikkaflee. "It's delicious!"

"It's one of their specialties," said Magdalena. "We call it monkey mango salad."

"Technically golden-hairs aren't monkeys," said

Merriweather, "but we rather liked the name. Have some, Evangeline, dear."

Evangeline decided that she *would* have some monkey mango salad.

Why not? she thought. *I've already been chewed on by a goat. Why not try fruit salad prepared by apes?*

She was taking her first bite when suddenly there was a commotion in the clearing.

Merriweather and Magdalena ran to the window of the hut and looked out.

"It's the golden-hairs!" Merriweather shouted. "But . . ."

"Good heavens!" cried Magdalena. "What are they doing?"

"I haven't the slightest idea," Merriweather replied, scratching his head. "Aphrodite, perhaps you could take a look."

Dr. Aphrodite Pikkaflee joined Merriweather and Magdalena at the window.

"Hmmmm," she said. "Perhaps it's some sort of mating ritual. I've never seen anything like it."

Evangeline peeked out the window.

"Look!" she cried. "There's Pansy!"

It was true. One of the golden-hairs—Evangeline thought it was the one who had carried her—was holding Pansy in his arms as he shuffled around in the circle.

"But what in tarnation are those apes up to?" asked Dr. Pikkaflee. "I just can't make it out."

Under normal circumstances, she wouldn't have used the word tarnation, but the golden-hairs were behaving so strangely that it got the better of her. To see them skipping about in a little circle and grinning idiotically was just too much for the primatologist. Occasionally, one of the golden-hairs would even hop in the middle of the circle as if he were trying to beat out the others.

"I know!" shouted Evangeline happily. "I know exactly what they're doing! It's simple! They're doing the goo-goo dance!"

Sure enough, Dadoo himself stepped into the clearing. His blowpipe was still in his hand, and his fingers were smeared with the green paste. Evangeline was right. The golden-hairs were goo-goo!

"Dadoo!" shouted Evangeline, running to her friend and touching foreheads. "Dadoo! You found us!"

"Evangelines!" Dadoo said, grinning so broadly that every single one of his pointed teeth was showing. "I finds you now! You greats! You really most extremely greats!"

Evangeline introduced Dadoo to her parents, who were astounded at the fact that their daughter was on a first-name basis with a headhunter.

"It's very nice to meet you, Mr. Dadoo," Merriweather said, extending his hand as if to shake it.

"We wrestles later," Dadoo said gravely. "Now we walks!"

Evangeline turned to Dr. Pikkaflee.

"What about Pansy?" she asked.

By now, the older golden-hair had put Pansy down. The young ape seemed to be enjoying herself immensely as she frolicked and imitated the others in the goo-goo dance.

"I think you know the answer to that question yourself, my dear," Dr. Pikkaflee replied kindly. "After all, this is Pansy's home."

Evangeline took one last look at Pansy. She knew that the apes in the clearing were not Pansy's actual mother and father, but she also knew that golden-hairs naturally belonged in the jungle. Besides, Pansy had made it clear where she wanted to be.

Evangeline remembered the way the little ape had looked for her parents as *The Flying Monkey* approached Ikkinasti.

"Goodbye," she called out. "Goodbye, Pansy!"

And then, without looking back, she followed her parents, Dr. Aphrodite Pikkaflee, and Dadoo into the jungle.

Just a few days ago, I was at Mudd's Manor, the girl thought as she marched along. *But now I am walking through the Ikkinasti Jungle with my parents, a primatologist who thought she was a capuchin monkey, and a friendly headhunter. How strange life is! Strange and wonderful!*

But a shadow began to fall across the girl's philosophy as with each step the party got closer to the clearing where Rexi was destroying the jungle, and it occurred to her that not everything about life was so wonderful. Sometimes there were problems, serious problems that needed one hundred percent of your attention.

There must be a way to stop him! she told herself. *There must be an answer!*

But no answer would come. It was like pushing against a door that had been bolted on the inside. Evangeline kept pushing. She kept pushing until her brain was exhausted.

Chapter 23

The Law of the Jungle

Evangeline was just about to give up thinking altogether when she saw something shimmer in the shadowy light of the jungle. She looked to her left, and there, between two trees, she saw it. It was a web! An enormous web! A web the size of a door!

Evangeline's heart began to beat wildly. *A spitting spider wove that web,* she told herself. *A spitting spider of the Ikkinasti Jungle.*

She was already soaked with perspiration from the heat of the jungle, but now it began to pour off her, running down her arms and legs and into her eyes like tributaries of a mighty jungle river.

Her fears were confirmed when Dadoo stopped and pointed to the web with his blowpipe.

"Be carefuls now," he said. "Spider away, but she come backs soon, and thens . . ."

Instead of finishing his sentence, Dadoo demonstrated his meaning by spitting a tremendous wad of headhunter spit onto a nearby tree trunk.

"Thens you can't see," he went on. "Thens spiders have fancy dinners."

To emphasize his point, he smacked his lips in such a way that made Evangeline grateful that he had given up the practice of headhunting.

"We goes now," Dadoo said. "Fasts."

Evangeline was about to follow Dadoo's instructions, but as she turned away, she felt a fluttering of air just over her left shoulder, as if someone were fanning her. She turned to see an enormous butterfly. It was heading straight into the center of the web.

"No!" Evangeline called out. "No!"

But before the second was over, the butterfly had become hopelessly entrapped.

The more it struggled, the more the helpless creature became enmeshed in the awful stickiness of the web. Its wings, which were the size of Evangeline's hands, were an iridescent blue. To the girl, it seemed that a piece of the sky had fallen and become trapped in the web.

"Stop!" she cried out to the others. "Stop! The butterfly is caught in the spider's web."

"Yes," said Dr. Aphrodite Pikkaflee. "But unfortunately, my dear, that's the law of the jungle."

"She's right, Evangeline," her parents agreed. 'That's the law of the jungle. Spiders trap butterflies."

Evangeline's heart came very close to breaking at that moment. Had her parents forgotten the story they had told her about the day she was born? Wasn't it true that she had been blessed by a butterfly on the very first day of her life? And now did they really expect her to walk away and do nothing just because it was the law of the jungle?

All of Evangeline's young life, she had tried to be a good citizen. Even during the terrible months at Mudd's Manor, when it would have been understandable if she had transgressed against the rules of what most people thought was acceptable for a girl her age, she tried to behave in a way that she could be proud of. No, as far as she knew, she had never broken a law in her life. But there is always a first time for everything. And for Evangeline this was it.

"You can do what you like," she said to the others. "But I am not going to stand by and let that butterfly

die. If I can't save the jungle from Rexi, I can at least save that butterfly from the spider. And if it means breaking the law of the jungle, then so be it."

Before the others could stop her, she ran up to the web, squeezed her eyes shut, took a huge breath, and stuck her hands into it right up to the elbow.

"Ugh!" she said aloud.

The web was much stickier than she had imagined. It clung to her fingers and arms as if it had been coated with glue. It was strong, too, stronger than twine. Try as she might, she couldn't break it. For an awful moment the girl considered the terrifying possibility that she too might get stuck in its powerful stands.

And, she thought somewhat belatedly, *Dadoo said the spider would come back soon!*

This realization gave Evangeline renewed energy. She pulled! She yanked! She knotted! She unknotted!

Eventually, her hands completely covered with the strands of the sticky web, Evangeline was able to pull the butterfly from its trap. When she released it, well away from the web, she saw that the tip of her finger and thumb were smudged with the iridescent blue dust from its wings. Tiny motes of the dust glistened in the light, and Evangeline now saw that they were not just shades of blue, but also greens—the color of emeralds and spring grass and sycamore leaves. There were reds, tulip reds and coral reds and all the reds of all the sunsets. There were yellows and purples and oranges and violets. There were even tiny motes of black—midnight black and the black of good garden soil and the shining black of the blackest cat. Evangeline gazed in wonder at the dust. For a brief moment it seemed to her that all the beauty in the entire world was made up of that dust.

"We goes now," said Dadoo. "We goes before spiders come back. She mads when she see hers web. Very, most extremely mads. We goes now!"

But they were stopped again by Evangeline herself, who cried out in surprise as the butterfly slowly beat the air, circling again and again over her head. She knew it was the same one, because its wings were smudged just where she had touched them to pull it from the web.

Dadoo, especially, seemed interested in the butterfly's behavior, but he said nothing and instead looked at Evangeline with an expression that she had not seen before.

"Oh, hello!" said the girl. "This time, please be careful where you fly. That spider web was disgusting!"

Naturally, the butterfly couldn't understand a word of what she was saying, and it flew off again into the jungle. But later, Evangeline felt a rush of air against her cheek, and when she looked to see what might have been the cause, she saw that the butterfly had returned.

Of course, the others noticed the butterfly as well. It would have been impossible not to, big and beautiful as it was.

"What do you make of it, Dadoo?" asked Dr. Pikkaflee.

"Simples," Dadoo replied. "Evangelines break law of jungle. Now magics happen. Big magics."

"What do you mean 'magics happen'?" said Evangeline.

"You helps the butterfly," said Dadoo. "Now the butterfly help you."

"Help me?" Evangeline asked. "How can a butterfly help me?"

"You waits," said Dadoo. "You waits and see."

Chapter 24

Flying Rats!

After hours of walking, the adventurers neared the spot where Rexi had been working his terrible scheme. Evangeline, the enormous blue butterfly still flitting about her, listened for the rumbling of the bulldozers, but try though she might, she was met only with silence.

"Perhaps the goo-goo juice lasted longer than you thought, Dadoo," she said hopefully.

But Dadoo said nothing. He seemed to be concentrating on something, looking first to the left and then to the right as he stepped deliberately along.

Eventually, the party found its way into the clearing. Magdalena and Merriweather gasped at the horror of what they saw. Though Evangeline had done her best to describe the terrible wound that Rexi was inflicting upon the jungle, the reality of the destruction was hundreds of times worse than it had been in their imaginations.

As for Rexi and his workers, they were nowhere to be seen. For Evangeline, the silence they left behind was the saddest thing she had ever heard. No birds. No monkeys. No insects. Nothing. Nothing at all.

"We'd better hurry," said Dr. Pikkaflee. "He's probably gone back to Bababun to get new bulldozers, but if I know my brother, he'll be back soon. He won't be satisfied until the entire jungle is gone."

No sooner had the five travelers reached the center of the clearing than a terrible yellow racket came bursting out on all sides of the jungle around them. Before they knew it, Dadoo, Dr. Pikkaflee, Magdalena, Merriweather, and Evangeline were surrounded by the bulldozers.

Rexi himself was driving one of the big yellow machines. Evangeline saw that he was wearing a pair of sunglasses, the mirrored kind. All of the drivers were wearing sunglasses, too, the exact same kind that Rexi had on. Evangeline also saw that in the bucket of each of the bulldozers there was a large metal box

about the size of a medium-sized television set.

There was no point in trying to escape. Just like the butterfly, they had fallen into a trap.

When the bulldozers had them surrounded in a tight circle, Rexi signaled the drivers to turn off their engines.

"Hellooooo down there!" he sang out nastily.

He was speaking through a bullhorn, which Evangeline thought was ridiculous, since they would have been able to hear him perfectly well without it.

Dr. Aphrodite Pikkaflee was the first to speak.

"Rexi!" she said. "What do you think you are doing?"

"What's the problem?" Rexi snarled through the bullhorn.

"The problem is you're tearing down the jungle!" Evangeline shouted up at him. "To make toothpicks!"

"So what?" Rexi hissed. "The world wants toothpicks, and I'm providing them. You should thank me for it."

"No, I shouldn't!" Evangeline answered angrily. "You're not thinking about the world. You're thinking about yourself! Yourself and your money!"

"So sue me," sneered Rexi. "Do you know how many toothpicks I can make from these trees? Do you? Well, get out your calculator, girlie, because the answer is plenty! Ple-e-e-e-n-n-n-ty! I'm going to be a zillionaire! Possibly even a gadillionaire! I'll be the toothpick king of the world thanks to this jungle."

"But what about all the animals who live here?" Evangeline cried. "What about the birds and the monkeys and the golden-hairs?"

"They can rent apartments in Huehuetenango for all I care," said Rexi. "It's not my fault if they decided to live here."

"But this is their home!" Evangeline shouted.

"Not anymore, missy," said Rexi. "Not anymore!"

"You bads man," said Dadoo. "You really most extremely terribles and bads.'"

"*I'm* bad?" Rexi replied, standing up in the seat of the bulldozer and rubbing his bottom. "You should talk. At least I don't go around with an oversized bean-shooter whooshing pointy things into people's behinds. By the way, I'd like to buy the recipe for that goo-goo stuff. It might come in handy someday."

"You're mad, Rexi!" said Merriweather. "Completely mad!"

"Sticks and stones," Rexi snapped. The way he curled his lip made him look like a weasel. "By the way, I thought the jungle would have gotten you by now."

"Well," said Magdalena, "think again."

"'Well,'" repeated Rexi, holding his nose and

imitating Magdalena in a horrible voice, "'think again.'"

Hearing Rexi talk to her mother like that was almost more than Evangeline could bear.

"I'll bet if I crawled up on that bulldozer and bopped you one on the nose, you'd cry like a baby," she said.

"I wouldn't try it," Rexi sneered.

But every single person there, including members of his own crew, saw him pull back even though he was sitting high above Evangeline on the seat of the bulldozer.

"Anyway," he continued, "it really doesn't make any difference."

"What are you talking about?" Evangeline said. "What do you mean that it doesn't make any difference?"

"What I mean," said Rexi, "is that I finally figured out that no matter what I try, Aphrodite will be in my way. That's why I started my toothpick business in the *middle* of the jungle. I figured by the time she found out about it, I'd be all the way to the edge, and by then it would be too late. But could she keep her big fat nose out of my business? Noooooooooooo! She's not going to stop me now, though, and neither are you, shorty. No one is!"

"And just what makes you so sure of that?" Aphrodite asked.

"Oh, nothing, really," Rexi replied. "Nothing at all except for the little presents that I have here for you and your friends."

Rexi pointed to the metal box that was in the bucket of his bulldozer.

"What's in the box?" asked Merriweather.

"In there?" Rexi tittered. "I'll give you a hint."

Rexi stood up in the seat and began to wave his arms around horribly. Without any warning, he let loose with a big gob of spit. It was disgusting.

"The spiders!" said Evangeline. "The spitting spiders of Ikkinasti!"

"What a clever girl you are," said Rexi, sitting down and wiping his chin. "Too bad I despise clever children. It's also too bad you don't have a pair of these special nifty sunglasses. You see, the spiders can look right at me, and not a thing will happen. They can spit all they want, and I'll still be able to see all the way from here to the gigantic swimming pool I'm going to build from all the toothpick money I'll make. But you? Well, you don't have any of these glasses, do you?"

"Shut your eyes, everybody!" said Aphrodite Pikkaflee. "Shut your eyes before he opens the boxes!"

"Shut them all you want," said Rexi. "You won't be able to keep them shut forever! You'll have to open them sometime, and when you do, we'll be right here!"

While Rexi had been delivering this last speech, the blue butterfly stopped circling Evangeline and slowly made its way toward Rexi, where it began to flutter around the wicked man's weasely face. Rexi batted at it again and again, but each time the butterfly darted away, only to return. Soon it was joined by another.

"Where are these disgusting bugs coming from?" Rexi asked, waving his stubby hands in front of his face. "Flying rats! That's what I call them. What a nuisance! The world will be well rid of them!"

But in the short time it had taken to utter those sentences, still more butterflies had arrived. And more! And more! In a matter of seconds, it was as if every butterfly in the jungle was flying around Rexi and the drivers. There were thousands of them! Tens of thousands. Huge butterflies. Tiny butterflies. Medium-sized butterflies. Each one different from the next. Some were a shimmering blue, like the one Evangeline had rescued from the spider web. Others

were lime green. Some were spotted. Some were striped. Their wings were pointed and scalloped and lacy and frilled. The air was a-whir with the beating of their wings.

Now, you and I both know that one butterfly isn't really scary. And ten butterflies aren't really scary. But thousands? Tens of thousands? Rexi was downright terrified. Not only that, he was so busy batting the air and flailing his arms that he couldn't get to the box.

Dadoo turned to Evangeline and beamed.

"You sees," he said. "Magics. You helps the butterfly. Now the butterfly help you."

"Get away from me!" Rexi was shouting. "Get away! Stop it! Help! Help!"

"We'd better get going while the going is good," said Dr. Pikkaflee.

The five travelers took one last look at Rexi and his crew and hurried to the other side of the clearing.

Just before they stepped back into the jungle, Evangeline looked back.

"The butterflies are gone!" she cried out.

It was true. The butterflies had almost completely disappeared, but Rexi and his men were now trying to fight off something even more powerful than thousands of butterflies.

"Look!" Evangeline shouted. "Look! Look!"

It was the golden-hairs! They came bursting through the clearing, heading straight for Rexi and his men. Evangeline watched as the biggest one ran to Rexi and snatched him up in his arms.

"Put me down, you fleabag!" Rexi shouted like a spoiled baby. "Put me down! I've got trees to knock over! Toothpicks to make!"

But the ape didn't put him down. In fact, now carrying Rexi as if he were a football, the golden-hair turned and ran back into the jungle. Just at the edge of the clearing, the ape grabbed a low hanging vine, swung up into the treetops, and began to brachiate, carrying Rexi into the heart of the jungle.

"Help!" they heard Rexi cry again. "Help! I'm getting seasick!"

By now, the other golden-hairs had joined the one who was carrying Rexi. Each of them carried one of the bulldozer crew. In a matter of seconds, they had all disappeared behind the green curtain of the jungle.

"I don't think we'll be seeing Rexi again for a long, long time," said Merriweather.

"Goodbye and good riddance," Magdalena added.

Evangeline, hoping to see if Pansy had joined the other golden-hairs on their escapade, continued to stare into the spot where the apes had swung into the jungle with Rexi and the others. She looked up just in time to see Dr. Aphrodite Pikkaflee wipe a tear from the corner of her eye.

"He's rotten to the core," she sniffed quietly, "but he *is* my brother."

Evangeline took Dr. Pikkaflee's hand. The woman's palms were as callused and hard as a golden-hair's from all those years of brachiating, but the backs were as soft as her own.

"Maybe Rexi and his men will like monkey tag," the girl said.

Chapter 25

The Ikkinasti Suite

Once the party reached Bababun, it was only a matter of days before it was time for Evangeline to leave Ikkinasti and return with her parents to the cozy bungalow in New England. Naturally, it was very difficult for the girl to say goodbye to Dadoo. After all, he was the only headhunter she had ever known.

They were standing on the path that led to the longhouse.

"Dadoo give present nows," he said.

For one anxious moment, Evangeline wondered if the present were going to be one of the trophies that hung in Dadoo's longhouse. But the girl needn't have worried. Dadoo took the blowpipe from his shoulder and slipped it over hers.

"Maybe you needs make goo-goo juice sometimes," the headhunter said.

Evangeline didn't know what to say. There was nothing *to* say. The blowpipe, she knew, was Dadoo's most treasured object. She turned to thank the headhunter, but he was gone. He had disappeared into the jungle just as suddenly as he had appeared from it on the day she met him.

"You greats!" the girl shouted into the green jungle air. "You really most extremely greats and wonderfuls!"

Later, as *The Flying Monkey* was heading back over the ocean, Evangeline asked Dr. Pikkaflee a question that had been bothering her almost since the day she had sat in Dadoo's longhouse while he and Dr. Pikkaflee talked.

"Dr. Pikkaflee," she said. "Where is Dadoo's family? Where are his wife and children? Where are his mother and father? Where are his brothers and sisters? And his nieces and nephews? Where are his second cousins, twice removed?"

"Evangeline, my dear," Dr. Pikkaflee replied, "I thought you knew. Dadoo is the last of his people. He has no wife and children. He has no mother and father. No second cousins, twice removed. They're gone."

"Gone?" the girl asked. "Where did they go?"

"Rexi is not the first person to try to destroy the jungle," she said. "And he won't be the last. Dadoo's people lived in the jungle. They were in the way. Dadoo is the only one left."

Evangeline didn't say another word all the way home.

When they got back to the cozy bungalow, Merriweather and Magdalena got to work immediately writing their book. They called it *You're It! Monkey Tag with the Golden-Haired Apes of the Ikkinasti Jungle*. It was an instant success and made loads of money, all of which Evangeline's parents donated to helping save the jungle from people like Rexi. In the book, they included the recipe for monkey mango salad. The trouble was it never tasted quite as good as it had in the clearing in the jungle. Magdalena became convinced that the golden-hairs had used a secret ingredient. Anyway, here it is, if you ever want to try it:

1 banana
1 mango
some coconut
some papaya
some pineapple
Peel everything.
Mix it all up and eat it with your fingers.
Best if served by a golden-haired ape of the Ikkinasti Jungle.

Dr. Aphrodite Pikkaflee decided that she would move back to Ikkinasti. She and Dadoo started a school so that the headhunter's knowledge about the jungle would not be lost. They called it Jungle U. They offer courses in everything from goo-goo juice to spiders. They even teach courses in Dadoo's language, and the classroom is alive with all kinds of people buzzing and clicking and humming. Dadoo turned out to be surprisingly effective in the classroom. Apparently, when your teacher is a headhunter, you do your homework.

As for Evangeline, she was terrifically happy to be home. Who wouldn't have been? She was especially happy on the days she received letters from Dr. Aphrodite Pikkaflee, who promised that she and Dadoo would come for a visit once affairs at Jungle U. calmed down.

But in spite of this good news, a cloud began to settle over Evangeline. She could not forget what Dr. Pikkaflee had told her about Dadoo when they were returning from Ikkinasti. She tried to imagine what it would be like to have no family, to be the very last one of your people, and she spent many hours sitting quietly in the treetops surrounding the cozy bungalow with Dadoo's blowpipe slung over her shoulder.

Naturally, Merriweather and Magdalena were greatly concerned to see their daughter so broken-hearted. It was especially difficult for Merriweather, but Magdalena, who was perhaps a bit wiser in these matters, reassured him.

"Don't forget, Merriweather, my darling," she would say. "Sadness is a part of life, too. There is not a single soul on this earth who has not been sad at one time or another. Evangeline will not stay sad forever."

Magdalena was right, of course. The cure for Evangeline's sadness came in the piano lessons that she resumed with Madame Valentina Kloudishskaya. As she practiced hour after hour, day after day, her grief began to soften until, eventually, it found its way out of her heart and into her fingers. Before long, the girl was composing music of her own.

Her first really big piece she called the *Ikkinasti Suite*. In it, she tried to recreate the sounds of her adventure in the jungle. There was a section right in the middle when she lifted her hands from the keyboard to create an eerie silence. This, of course, represented what Rexi had done to the jungle.

"Zat girl is a musical che-e-e-nius," Madame Kloudishskaya told her parents. "I knew it ze minute I zaw her."

There was also a part where Evangeline pounded the big, rumbling bass keys for three minutes straight. You can probably guess that this was the sound of the bulldozers.

But Evangeline's favorite part was the very end, when she would jump up from the bench and play the *strings* of the piano like a harp. Measure after measure, she strummed, until the very air vibrated with undertones and overtones and all tones in between. Evangeline wouldn't stop until it seemed that the music had taken flight and was supporting itself on thousands upon thousands of delicate, brightly colored wings.

Of course, this music quickly found its way into the hearts of all the people in Evangeline's circle—her mother and father, Madame Kloudishkaya, Dr. Aphrodite Pikkaflee, Dadoo. And like all works of the imagination whose main ingredient is love, it acted as a great connector, linking them to one another and to Evangeline herself, no matter how far away she traveled or what other adventures she had.

EVANGELINE MUDD'S
ADVENTURES CONTINUE IN

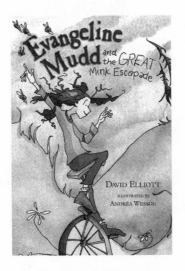

*Evangeline Mudd and
the Great Mink Escapade.* . . .

Chapter 1

URGENT!!!

I wonder if you can imagine how Evangeline Mudd felt on the day this story begins. After all, not so long ago, she had been whisked through a jungle in the arms of a four-hundred-pound ape. She'd rubbed noses with a headhunter. Why, she had even broken the Law of the Jungle. But now all that was over. Now she was home, safe and sound with her parents at their cozy bungalow in New England.

It wouldn't be fair to say that Evangeline was unhappy. After all, she had spent most of her time away wishing that she *could be* home. It's just that, well, now she had a great deal in common with those kids in countries where parents give them slices of pineapple sprinkled in red-hot chili pepper.

An excerpt from *Evangeline Mudd and the Great Mink Escapade*

The first time those kids have that snack, their eyes practically bug out of their heads. Their faces turn pink, then maroon, and then a lovely shade of vermilion. Tears stream from their eyes. "Call a doctor!" they holler as they run in circles, looking for buckets of water to dunk their heads in. "Call the police! Call the fire department!"

But then, after the hullabaloo has died down and the pineapple is gone, and the kids are back to normal, the strangest thing happens. "Please," the kids say to their parents, "give us more."

Yes, Evangeline was very much like those children. In other words, she had had one adventure, and she was dying to have another.

On the afternoon in question, the sunlight was filtering through the canopy of the trees, dappling the leaves in a way that made them seem like the feathers of a fantastic bird. Evangeline was brachiating, hand over hand, in a stand of maples that grew behind the cozy bungalow. (Brachiating, by the way, is how monkeys and apes get around in this world—by swinging from one branch to another. Evangeline was an expert brachiator.)

This is terrific, she thought as she reached for a branch just over her head. *But it would be so much better if I were being chased by a gorilla.*

An excerpt from *Evangeline Mudd and the Great Mink Escapade*

She was just about to do a double flip when she heard her mother calling from below.

Magdalena's voice was such that no matter how loudly she spoke, she seemed to be reciting the sweetest poetry. This was especially true when she was speaking to Evangeline.

"Perhaps you'd better come down now, dear. The mail has just arrived. There's a letter for you."

A letter! Evangeline landed on the next limb with both feet. Hugging the maple's smooth trunk as if it were a long-lost friend, she scrambled her way to the ground.

The letter could be from only one person. Dr. Aphrodite Pikkaflee, the world's most famous

An excerpt from *Evangeline Mudd and the Great Mink Escapade*

primatologist and the very person with whom Evangeline had had her adventure in the jungle! Dr. Pikkaflee had already written Evangeline several letters telling her of the progress she was making with the jungle school she had started.

Evangeline opened her arms as wide as she could and ran to her mother. Her intention, naturally, was to hug the woman. But this wasn't as easy as you might think. At present, Magdalena was as round as a beach ball. Evangeline would have a brother or sister very soon.

"Where's the letter from Dr. Pikkaflee?" Evangeline asked, her arms encircling what they could of her mother's generous middle.

"It's on the kitchen table, darling. Right next to the gooseberry jam." Magdalena picked at her daughter's scalp exactly the way a golden-haired ape mother might do.

Evangeline let go of Magdalena and ran toward the house.

"But the letter isn't from Dr. Pikkaflee, dear," her mother called out.

Evangeline stopped in her tracks. If it wasn't from Dr. Aphrodite Pikkaflee, then who could it be from? Evangeline wasn't the kind of girl who got a lot of letters. After all, she was only ten years old.

An excerpt from *Evangeline Mudd and the Great Mink Escapade*

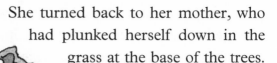

She turned back to her mother, who had plunked herself down in the grass at the base of the trees. "The return address says Eversharp," Magdalena said. A hummingbird flew around her head, momentarily mistaking her reddish curls for a bouquet of snapdragons. "Miss B. Eversharp."

Evangeline wracked her brain. "But I've never heard of someone named B. Eversharp," she said at last.

"Are you sure?" her mother asked, smiling at the hummingbird. "She certainly seems to have heard of you, because on the back of the letter, B. Eversharp has written URGENT in big black letters and has punctuated it with three exclamation points."

At this, the hummingbird zoomed up into the trees.

Now, if you ever get a letter from a stranger marked URGENT, your heart should start to speed up a bit because URGENT usually means one of two things. One: You owe someone a great deal of money, and she wants you to pay it back as soon as possible.

An excerpt from *Evangeline Mudd and the Great Mink Escapade*

As far as she knew, Evangeline didn't owe any money, except five cents to the local library for a book she had returned one day late. She couldn't imagine that the librarian would send her a letter with URGENT written on the back, and certainly not URGENT followed by three exclamation points. Besides, the librarian's name was Emanuel Bopp, not Miss B. Eversharp.

That meant that this was the second kind of URGENT, the kind where someone is in terrible trouble and needs help. And naturally, if that kind of urgent is written in big black letters and is followed by not one but *three* exclamation points, well, then, it probably means that you must take action immediately.

Evangeline turned toward the house and ran as if she *were* being chased by a gorilla, for *action* is a word that is very closely related to another, and that word, of course, is *adventure*.